Falling Hard

by Megan Sparks

capstone
young readers

Roller Girls is published in the United States by
Capstone Young Readers
A Capstone Imprint
1710 Roe Crest Drive
North Mankato, Minnesota 56003
www.capstoneyoungreaders.com

First published in 2013 by Curious Fox,
an imprint of Capstone Global Library Limited,
7 Pilgrim Street, London, EC4V 6LB
Registered company number: 6695582
www.curious-fox.com

Text © Hothouse Fiction Ltd 2013
Series created by Hothouse Fiction
www.hothousefiction.com
The author's moral rights are hereby asserted.

Library of Congress Cataloging-in-Publication Data is available on the
Library of Congress website.
ISBN: 978-1-62370-023-2 (paper-over-board)
ISBN: 978-1-62370-021-8 (hardcover)

Summary: When Annie moves from London to small town Illinois, the last
thing she expects to do is to join the Roller Derby team.

Cover original design: www.spikyshooz.com
Photo: Getty Images/Vetta
Designer: Russell Griesmer, Kay Fraser

With special thanks to Alexandra Diaz

Printed in China by Nordica.
0413/CA21300517
032013   007226NORDF13

Roller Girls

Falling Hard

Chapter 1

A doorbell ringing in the middle of the night usually meant bad news. Annie Turner squinted at the unfamiliar clock.

11:46. Something had to be wrong. There was something definitely wrong. She looked at the clock again.

11:46.

A.M.

Then it all came back to her: the long and delayed flight from Heathrow to O'Hare, then the wrong turn her "I know the way" dad took that put them in Indiana. It wasn't until four in the morning that they had arrived at their real destination: Liberty Heights, Illinois. By that point, Annie couldn't do the math to work out what time it was in London.

Ding-dong. The doorbell. Again. She tumbled out of bed and went in search of the front door.

Dad, with his brown hair sticking up to one side, met her in the hall. He looked as disoriented as she felt.

He pointed to the front door and opened it with a flourish. The brilliant sunlight burst into Granny and Grandpa's old house. Dad cowered and said in his Transylvanian vampire accent, "Argh, eet burns!"

Annie would have rolled her eyes at him if she wasn't squinting and holding her own hand out in front of her. It took several seconds to realize someone was standing outside. Two someones.

One was a petite woman with perfectly cropped blond hair wearing a pressed light-blue shirt and white linen pants. Next to her was a tall girl around Annie's age with wild brown ringlets that matched her skin. She sported a cool 1950s orange bowling shirt and real tattered jeans, not the kind bought that way. The two didn't look like they belonged in the same universe, let alone on the same doorstep. Only their hazel eyes were the same.

Oh, no. People. Annie should have remembered doorbells were usually rung by people and at least put on a dressing gown. Instead she stood there in her faded Winnie-the-Pooh nightie — the one that should have gone to the charity shop years ago but was so comfy she couldn't part with it.

The girl's wearing cool vintage clothes and I'm in Pooh. She must think I'm four instead of fourteen, Annie thought.

"Hi!" said the woman in a chipper voice. "I'm Marilyn Jones and this is my daughter, Lexie. Welcome to the neighborhood."

"Thanks. I'm David, and that's Annie," Dad said, yawning. Annie could tell he was having a hard time waking up.

Mrs. Jones smiled, showing her perfect white teeth. "I work for the real estate agency and I have the keys to the diner down on Main Street you're renting."

Dad perked up immediately as he took the keys from her hand. "Old Al's. I'm turning it into a café."

"What a wonderful idea. Al's has been empty for so long — we were delighted to find a tenant." The woman thrust a basket into Annie's arms. "We brought these as a little welcome to Liberty Heights. They're blueberry muffins."

"Annie's favorite, huh, Beanie?" Dad said.

Annie wanted to pull her Winnie-the-Pooh nightie over her head and disappear. Did Dad have to call her that in front of the new neighbors? Ever since she grew about a foot last year, and became too tall for gymnastics, Dad had been teasing her with a new nickname.

String Bean.

"Thanks," Annie said to Mrs. Jones. She'd deal with Dad later. "That's lovely."

Mrs. Jones clapped her hands in glee. "Ooh,

Lexie, did you hear her accent? *Lovely*. Isn't it the cutest?"

"Mo-om," Lexie said under her breath. She gave Annie an apologetic look, which Annie greatly appreciated. She liked Lexie already.

Mrs. Jones turned to Dad. "But you don't seem to have much of a British accent."

"Wha-aat?" Dad looked at her in shock.

No, Dad. Please don't do your cockney accent. It's horrid, Annie pleaded silently. *Please don't do it.*

"'Ave oi los' me accent, 'ave oi?" He sounded like Dick Van Dyke in *Mary Poppins*.

Annie covered her eyes with her hand, though the sun wasn't to blame this time.

Seeing that he'd embarrassed his daughter enough, Dad put his arm around her and returned to his normal voice. "I grew up here, in this very house," he said. He nodded at the faded, floral wallpaper. "Still looks pretty much the same, in fact. I met Annie's mom in London when I was a student."

Mrs. Jones peered over their shoulders. "Is she awake? I'd love to meet her."

Annie and her dad looked at each other. Right now Mum was probably at work at her law firm, even though it was Saturday. Without Annie and

Dad living there anymore, Mum might never come home from work.

A knot tightened in Annie's stomach.

Dad squeezed Annie's shoulders and kissed the top of her head. "Philippa is staying in London."

Mrs. Jones's eyes widened as she understood what Dad was saying. "Oh, I'm sorry. Well, if you need anything, *anything*, you just let us know, okay?"

Dad assured her they would as Lexie grabbed her mother by the elbow. "We should go. They need to unpack and stuff."

They all waved goodbye. Lexie mouthed, *Sorry*. Annie grinned in return. Definite friend potential.

Dad closed the door before wrapping Annie in a hug and kissing her forehead. Annie pressed her head into his chest.

"I'm glad you're here with me," Dad said.

"Me too," Annie said and squeezed him tighter. Dad had always been the one there for her while Mum worked as a lawyer; Annie couldn't imagine living without him. On the other hand, it was going to be weird living without Mum. It had been the hardest decision she'd ever had to make.

Dad must have known what she was thinking.

"We'll call your mom in a bit. Tell her we're here

and all. But first," he said, dangling the keys Mrs. Jones had brought, "let's check out Rosie Lee's."

"Yes!" Annie said. It had been her idea to call the café Rosie Lee's, which was cockney rhyming slang for tea. A reminder of home so far away. "But I want to shower and get dressed first."

Dad rolled his eyes and gave an exasperated sigh. "Girls. Always want to look their best."

Annie mimicked him. "Dads. Always in a hurry."

She ran a hand through her brown hair slowly and examined her fingernails for a few seconds while Dad tapped his foot impatiently. With a laugh, she dropped the act and sprinted to the shower. She was as eager to see the new café as he was.

For years, Dad had impressed family and friends with his cooking and baking. He never followed a cookbook, and yet he always seemed to know just how much to use and what flavors went together. When he'd seen on the internet that his old hangout,

Al's, was up for lease, he'd decided it was finally time to put his kitchen skills to use.

"Growing up, Al's was the bomb," Dad said as they walked down to the café eating Mrs. Jones's muffins. "My friends and I used to go there after basketball games for burgers and milkshakes. I even kissed a girl or two in the corner booth." He paused for a second. "No, wait, that only happened to the other guys."

Annie listened to his stories as she checked out the small city. There was so much space! Every house they passed was detached and had a large front and back garden. Still, kids played on the quiet streets, moving out of the way when an occasional car drove along. Main Street, just a few blocks from her grandparents' house, with its rows of shops, had more traffic, but mostly just people looking for a place to park.

Outside the diner formerly known as Al's, Dad took a deep breath. "Wow, it's exactly how I remember."

Glass lined the whole front of the diner, and a black and white canopy offered shade over the pavement in front of it. It looked cool and inviting. On nice days like today, Annie could imagine people sitting at tables enjoying a cream tea with scones and strawberry jam.

"Here," Dad said, handing Annie the keys. "You do the honors."

She drew out the moment, building the suspense, before finally turning the lock to the soon-to-be Rosie Lee's.

Then she gasped. The sight inside was enough to make Annie wish they could run back to London. The photos they had seen online, which made the place look retro and fun, hadn't been taken recently.

At least three different bug species scurried across the floor as Dad and Annie took tentative steps. Mouse droppings covered the greasy counters. The booths were gone (probably a good thing, or they'd be mouse mansions) and the floor looked raw and naked. Dust, dirt, and grime covered everything. The glass display case housed so much mold it looked like it had been taken over by a furry green monster.

Annie shuddered. If they were eaten alive by mold or insects, how long would it take for someone to discover their remains?

Dad ran a hand through his brown hair, making it stand straight up like it had this morning. "Let's not tell your mom how bad it is. I don't want to hear her say, 'I told you so.'"

Annie nodded. That was exactly what Mum would say. When Mum had found out he wanted to open a café, she'd said food businesses were a waste of money.

Annie didn't know if Dad was finally following his dreams or rebelling against Mum when he decided to rent his old hangout sight unseen. Either way, Annie couldn't bear to see her dad fail. He was a fabulous baker and if Mrs. Jones's gooey and tasteless muffins were any indication of the rest of the town's cooking, he'd be an instant hit.

Annie took a deep breath. This had been a fun place to be, once upon a time. So what if Dad rushed into getting the place? It was still pretty cool. And cheap. They could fix it up and make it exactly what they wanted it to be.

It was going to rock.

Eventually.

"Well," Annie said. "Let's get started." She found an old boom box in the kitchen and turned it on, tuning through the stations until she found one playing The Clash.

Dad grabbed a broom and was soon half

sweeping, half singing into it as a microphone. When he'd lived in Liberty Heights, Dad not only played basketball, but was also in a garage band. The photos of Dad as a head-banging teen with long hair always made Annie laugh. Still, it was listening to his old CD collection that had given Annie her taste for classic rock, especially punk.

"I'm so glad you're here," Dad said between broom-guitar solos. "It'll be good for you to finally experience life in the States."

"I've visited Granny and Grandpa in Florida loads of times, remember?" Annie teased as she sprayed cleaner on the front windows.

"Trust me, Liberty Heights is nothing like Disney World and retirement communities. We don't go around with mouse ears here."

Annie squirted some spray in his direction. "I was five when I did that, and you bought a pair too."

"Rubbish," Dad said in a hoity-toity voice.

"So what is there to do in Liberty Heights? Besides clean and help out in this fab place?" Annie added quickly.

Dad looked at her mischievously. "I was hoping, now that you're too big for the uneven bars, you might enjoy basketball, like me. You're tall enough."

True. At five foot eleven (and a half), she was one of the tallest girls at her old school. But basketball? The last time she played netball during PE, the ball almost broke her nose. It was one thing to do a cartwheel on the balance beam. It was completely different to try catching a ball while running.

Dad set down the broom and leaned into it. "Well, how about cheerleading? It's kind of like gymnastics."

"Cheerleading might be fun. The routines they show on TV seem cool." Annie finished with the windows and threw away the dirty paper towels. Then she stepped back to look through the windows. The difference was astonishing. Looking through the clean windows, everything on the outside seemed to sparkle. On the inside . . . well, it still needed a lot of work.

Like attacking the green monster in the display case. Mum would have called a professional cleaning team or thrown the whole case away. But Dad wasn't going to give up that easily. First, he sprayed it with bleach. "This way it won't bite back," he said. Then he pretended to wrestle it out of the display case. Once it was gone, lying dead in the trash, they disinfected the case again. No mercy.

After several hours, the place was beginning to shape up. Dad straightened his back with a few loud pops. Annie could feel a blister forming on her hands from all the scrubbing.

Dad groaned as other parts of his body creaked. "Why don't you take a break?" he suggested. "Check out the downtown area, if you want." He paused for a moment and added, "And remember to look both ways. Cars drive on the right here."

Annie didn't need to be told twice. The sun was still shining and she couldn't wait to learn more about the place she'd be spending the next year.

She kissed her dad on the cheek. "Don't work too hard," she told him. Then she raced back to the house.

Her Rollerblades were easy to find; she had placed them in her carry-on luggage so they wouldn't get lost. The clothes she had put on to clean in were dirty and sweaty, so she changed to the first things she could find: a Sex Pistols T-shirt and jeans.

Then she pulled her long brown hair into a ponytail and was ready to roll.

She surveyed her new room. It needed work, but it could wait a little while. When she got back, she'd unpack and start thinking about how to change the old-fashioned bedroom that had once been Aunt Julie's into something a bit cooler.

Outside, taking a deep breath of the fresh air, Annie felt great. Jetlag? No idea what that was. Sore hands from cleaning? Not anymore. The sun beat down on her and there was a breeze coming from the river, making it the perfect rollerblading temperature.

Annie whizzed past Rosie Lee's and checked out the rest of the downtown. It didn't take too long. Post office, pizza place, drug store, a few shops, the usual. Nothing like the hustle and bustle of London.

She passed a small playground with swings and a slide, worlds away from Hyde Park, where she and her friends had spent hours rollerblading.

Still, Dad had said Chicago was only a two-hour drive away.

It'll be great, living here, she thought, trying to convince herself.

She did crossovers as she turned a corner. A

loose shaggy black dog darted right in front of her. Too close to stop, too sudden to think, Annie leaped over the knee-high mutt. She cleared him easily, but when she landed on the other side, the skates almost shot out from under her.

Almost. Crouching low and waving her arms, she managed to keep her balance.

Phew, that was lucky. Annie straightened up and glanced at the dog. But as she turned, a blond girl suddenly stepped out of a frozen yogurt shop, and Annie crashed right into her. Annie, the girl, and her large frozen yogurt landed hard on the pavement.

Well, some of the frozen yogurt landed on the pavement. The rest covered the girl's blazer and miniskirt. "You idiot!" the blond girl screamed, looking down her front at the mess.

"Sorry, so sorry." Annie got back on her skates and offered the girl a hand. "Are you all right? I didn't see you. Or the dog. I'm really, really sorry."

"You should be." The girl refused Annie's hand and got up slowly on her own. "You could have killed me. And my clothes are totally ruined, thanks to you."

Annie knew the blazer and skirt could be washed, but she still felt bad. "I really am so sorry," she said quietly. She dug out a tissue from her pocket (she was pretty sure it was clean) and offered it to the girl. "Can I get you another frozen yogurt? I'm really sorry."

The girl swatted the tissue away with a look of disgust. "*Sorry*. Is that all you can say — *sorry?*" Every time the girl said "sorry" she said it in a very bad English accent. "If you're really *sorry*, why don't you go back where you came from?"

Annie didn't know what to say. She thought Americans were supposed to be friendly, like Mrs. Jones. Obviously this girl hadn't read the American Stereotypes Handbook.

Annie was saved from apologizing again by two brown-haired girls coming out of the shop. "Oh my god, Kelsey. Are you okay? Can you believe her? Totally could have killed you." The two new girls gave Annie the dirtiest look before helping their friend into a gold Volvo SUV and peeling away.

Annie squatted down on her skates and cringed. At this rate, she'd have offended every girl in town by the end of the day.

Something furry brushed up against her. Startled, Annie looked down to find the mutt mopping up the yogurt from the pavement. From the dog's neck hung a black leash and a skull-shaped tag with the name "Sid."

She picked up the leash. "Sid, huh?" she said. "We'd better find your owner. I don't think you'd fit in at Granny and Grandpa's." She laughed, thinking about what Dad would say if she brought Sid back to Granny and Grandpa's house, with its doilies and lace curtains and knick-knacks on every surface.

A tall, black-haired skater boy about her age ollied and grinded the curb in front of her. He wore black-and-white-checked Converse, black skinny jeans, and a plaid flannel shirt over a black Ramones T-shirt. Good taste. And cute too.

He flipped the skateboard into his hands and blew his hair out from his bright blue eyes. "Sorry 'bout that," he said. "Sid Vicious doesn't know any manners."

Annie looked down at the human Sid Vicious on her shirt, then at the dog, and laughed — they were nothing alike. She handed the skater boy the leash with a grin. "I take it Sid's yours, then?"

The boy took the dog's leash and wrapped it around his hand. "Not that he knows it. I just got him yesterday from the pound. So far, he only responds to food."

Sid jerked his head up, gave the air a quick sniff, and seemed to decide that the yogurt-flavored pavement was still his best bet. Annie laughed. "What does he like best?"

"Sid here doesn't discriminate," the skater said with a grin. "This morning he stole my mom's toast and gulped it down like it was bacon."

Sid had his nose in the air again. There was no yogurt left on the pavement to hold his attention.

Further down the street, a little boy was walking with his dad, eating a big bag of chips and leaving a trail of crumbs in his wake. Sid sniffed his next snack. The skater boy threw his board down and jumped on it just as Sid took off. The poor guy was nearly swept off his skateboard. Nearly. Instead, the board did some kind of flip and his feet landed squarely back on it.

"Thanks for your help," he called over his shoulder. "You got some sweet moves. You should be a roller girl."

"Pardon?" Annie asked. But Sid Vicious the dog and the cute skater boy were gone in a second.

It was time to head home. She was sore and her hands were sticky. Her American-culture crash course was over for the day.

Chapter 2

Annie woke up the next morning with a feeling of dread. It was the first day of school. Her first day at an American high school.

Annie just hoped the teen dramas she saw on TV really were fictitious. They didn't really put Kick Me signs on the new kids, did they? Students didn't really turn into vampires, hopefully, and not everyone would be expected to drive a fancy car and carry a thousand-dollar purse.

Dad wouldn't send her there if she'd be in any real danger, right?

She got out of bed and stretched with her arms in the air before folding over and resting her hands by her feet. Then she sat with her legs stretched out on either side on the faded pink carpet and leaned over her left leg. That felt good. She leaned over to the other side and let out a big breath.

Amazing how some simple stretches could relax her. Maybe because they had been such a huge part of her life.

Stretching and gymnastics were my whole *life,* Annie thought. For ten years, she had trained five days a week and had meets every weekend. Annie had loved it, especially the thrill of competing. She was really going to miss it.

She could see if there were any training studios nearby — maybe they'd let her work out on the equipment just to keep in shape. Could be fun.

Or could just be depressing, she thought, *knowing that I can't compete anymore.*

Maybe it was time for a change. To reinvent herself. New country, new interests, new life. Cheerleading, like Dad suggested. That could be fun. It'd be a change, if anything.

"Ann-nie," Dad called in a high-pitched American southern accent. "Y'all best git down here before this here breakfast goes and gets cold, y'hear?"

"Be there jus' as soon as I get mah duds on," she said in a cowboy accent that was probably just as bad as her dad's. Playing with accents had always been a favorite game of theirs. Good to know some things hadn't changed. Though, remembering the cockney accent he did in front of Lexie and her mum, maybe change was good.

Her open suitcases were still spread over the room. She hadn't had time to unpack yet; she and Dad had been too busy shopping for restaurant supplies, school supplies, and everyday-life supplies. She looked at her clothes and sighed.

What do people wear to school here? she thought.

She had always worn a uniform to school in London, but according to Dad, here she could wear anything. Within reason, of course.

Annie reached into the nearest suitcase. The first things she found were her old leotards. She had given away the ones that were too small before she left London, but couldn't bring herself to get rid of all of them. It was always possible she'd find some use for them. Part of a costume, maybe, but definitely not for school.

She tried on a T-shirt, skinny jeans, and her turquoise Converse — her "uniform" when she wasn't at school or the gymnasium — but it wasn't right. Not for the first day. Too scruffy.

"First impressions last forever," Mum always said.

She found the yellow summer dress Mum bought her before she left and put it on with some white ballet flats. Big improvement. For one thing, the dress showed off her long legs and if the sun kept shining, maybe her legs would soon be tan.

In the kitchen, Dad had prepared a full English breakfast: bacon, eggs, sausages, tomatoes, and fried bread. The smell reminded Annie of everything she'd left behind: Mum, London, home.

Dad waved his hands at the food. "Eat, eat. You're too skinny."

Annie picked up a triangle of fried bread and dipped the end into the egg yolk. She nibbled on the corner. "It's gorgeous, really. I just . . ."

Annie sighed, unable to eat much more with her stomach in knots.

Dad kissed her on the top of her head. "I know, Beanie. A lot has happened in a short amount of time and new schools are always scary. But it'll be fine. I'll take you to school. Go with you to the office. Just like I've done before on your other first days."

Except the last time Annie started a new school, she was eleven. It was time to do it on her own. "Thanks, but I think I'd rather go by myself."

Any other time Dad would have put on an accent and demanded to know whether he was cool enough to be seen with his daughter. She loved that about him: he was funny and messed around a lot, but he always knew when she needed him to be serious.

"Okay. You remember the way? We drove by it yesterday. And take your new phone, just in case you need to call."

Annie smiled. "Now you're sounding like Mum."

"Surely not!" he said in Mum's clipped tones.

Annie took a small bite of tomato. Then she picked up her new bag, making sure she had her phone turned to silent in the front pocket.

At the door, Annie turned around. Her dad was watching her, a fork-speared sausage held in the air.

"I'll come to Rosie Lee's after school. And Dad, try not to burn the place down." She smiled and left before Dad could think of a comeback.

Outside, any confidence she had faked disappeared. Maybe she should have let Dad take her. Hold her hand as they walked into the high school.

No, she could do this. Just like that time they mixed up the music for her floor routine, playing the theme song to *Chariots of Fire* instead of the White Stripes' "Seven Nation Army." She did her routine anyway and placed second. She could go to school alone and survive.

Up ahead, Annie caught sight of a familiar head of wild brown curls. Lexie. The other day she'd seemed nice. Was she really, or was that just because her mum was there? "Lexie," Annie called. Nothing. But there was a definite bob to Lexie's head. She was listening to music.

Annie jogged to catch up and tapped Lexie on the shoulder.

Lexie turned and broke into a huge smile. "Hey, good to see you again." She took the headphones out of her ears.

"Yes, likewise. I'm a bit nervous, though," Annie said.

Lexie scrunched up her nose. "School's not my favorite place either."

"Is that why you were playing 'Highway to Hell?'" Annie teased.

Lexie looked at her in surprise. "You like AC/DC?"

"I prefer more punk," Annie said, "but hard rock is good too."

Lexie nodded her approval. "We really should hang out. C'mon, I'll show you where to get your schedule."

Annie let out a breath she didn't know she had been holding. "Cheers. I love your clothes, by the way."

Today Lexie wore a denim jacket covered in cool buttons that read things like "Be yourself, everyone else is taken" — that one was an Oscar Wilde quote, Annie knew — and "eARTh," among others. Under the jacket was a lacy green shirt, and she also wore a long, hot-pink skirt, and tan cowgirl boots. Tied around the base of her wild hair was a purple scarf.

"Thanks," Lexie said, looking down at her outfit. "I buy everything at thrift stores. Mom hates it. She says the clothes are dirty and only poor people shop there. She wishes I could be preppier. But I don't like looking like everyone else."

Annie nodded. "The first time Mum saw my Sex Pistols T-shirt, she threatened to burn it," she said. She smoothed out her new dress. "Do you think I look all right?"

"*I* think you look fine," Lexie said. "But you should know, image is a huge thing at this school." She pointed. They were already nearing the building.

A flashy red car zoomed right by them, turned the corner quickly, and screeched to a stop inches before crashing into the parked car in front of it. Its driver got out and locked the doors with the remote in his hands, making the car beep twice and its lights flash. Mum's car did that too, but the driver of this car made Annie gasp for air. "Is he for real?"

Lexie rolled her eyes. "I know, right? Just because he can drive he thinks he's all hot."

But that wasn't what Annie meant. The only

time she'd seen a guy that good-looking in the flesh was when she and her friends went to the Abercrombie & Fitch store in London where they have live models walking around.

This guy didn't have to *think* he was hot, he *was* hot. Perfect blond hair fell across his forehead, making Annie long to brush it back. His light-blue shirt hung off his broad shoulders, showing off his tanned, toned arms, and his jeans fit like they were custom-made for him.

As he walked toward the school, he took off his sunglasses. He was close enough for Annie to see his startlingly green eyes. Were they contact lenses? Surely that color didn't occur in nature.

She watched him as he trotted up the steps and high-fived a group standing by the doors. *He's obviously very popular*, Annie thought. *Must have a million girls chasing him.*

Lexie broke her out of her reverie. "C'mon, I'll take you to the office and show you to your first class." Lexie took her by the arm and led her away.

Good thing, too, Annie thought. *Any more staring and I might start drooling.*

She got her schedule and immediately showed it to Lexie. Back in England she would have been starting her GCSEs, studying subjects based on what career she wanted. Here it seemed they wanted her to know a little of everything.

Lexie's eyes widened. "Wow, you're in a lot of advanced classes."

Annie shrugged. She never got poor marks but was hardly top of her class either. "British school system, I guess. We start younger, I think. Are you in any of my classes?"

"Are you kidding? I'm not really into school as long as I pass. As soon as I'm done here, I'm off to New York for art."

Lexie pointed to Annie's class and waved before heading to her own. Annie went through the door as if it were going to bite. She knew not to sit in the front, but the back was crowded with a group of kids, including, Annie groaned inside, Yogurt Girl from the other day. Kelsey or something. She slipped into a middle-row desk and wished for invisibility.

The English teacher, Ms. Schwartz, was fiftyish with dyed hair in various shades of brown and red with a few whisks of gray sticking straight out like television aerials. She wore a hemp blouse and canvas trousers. Annie had never had such a Bohemian-looking teacher.

"Okay, class, I have two very exciting announcements. First, we're starting Dickens's *A Tale of Two Cities*." There was a loud moan from the class. Annie wasn't worried; she'd read it last year. Hopefully she remembered it well enough not to have to read it again.

"And," Ms. Schwartz continued, "we have our very own Londoner with us this year — Annie Turner. Can you come up here, dear?"

Now Annie *was* worried. She heard whispers from the back of the room that sounded a bit like "yogurt" and "idiot."

Why do teachers always insist on humiliating their pupils? she thought.

She slid out of her chair and shuffled up to the front. With a deep breath, she looked up and faced the class.

As she expected, Kelsey was giving her the evil eye, but what she hadn't expected was to see the gorgeous guy from the parking lot. Unlike Kelsey, he seemed eager to hear what she had to say.

"Why don't you tell us about London? Last time I was there was just after Charles and Di got married. It must have changed so much since then," Ms. Schwartz said.

Yes, Annie was sure it had. Except she hadn't even been born that decade so she couldn't say what had changed. "What would you like to know?"

Immediately questions started flying and Ms. Schwartz, enjoying the excitement, didn't do anything to gain control.

Annie answered all of the questions, but her answers weren't what she really wanted to say.

"Do you know the Queen?" one girl asked.

Yes, we have tea every weekend. "No, but my mum's met the Prime Minister," Annie answered.

"Is it true that Scottish men don't wear anything under their kilts?" a red-headed girl asked, winking.

Aye, so best stay clear if there's a breeze. "I've never checked," Annie said.

"Do you drink tea, like, all the time?" a boy asked.

Of course not. We stop once in a while to sleep. "We do like tea, yes," Annie responded, "but we drink other stuff too, of course, like fizzy drinks and squash."

The sound the class made was a combination between "huh" and "ew." Obviously "squash" didn't translate well. She just hoped the American meaning wasn't rude. Annie was about to explain that squash was a concentrated fruit drink when Kelsey spoke up.

"Is granny chic, like, a really popular look in London?" Kelsey said, looking at Annie's new dress with a smirk. A few other girls sniggered.

Before Annie could retort with a clever comeback (one she hadn't thought up yet), Ms. Schwartz spoke up. "Okay, that's enough. Kelsey, let's not be rude. Annie, you can sit down, thanks."

Annie didn't have to be told twice. She rushed to her seat, both embarrassed and upset.

She liked her dress and she wasn't going to stop liking it because someone insulted it.

Especially someone like Kelsey.

When the bell rang, Annie gathered her things, wondering if she would be able to find her next class on her own. She noticed someone alongside her and blinked a couple of times. The gorgeous guy was there. Right next to her.

"Hey," he said.

Talking to her.

"Hey," Annie repeated, looking up into his green eyes. That seemed like a good response. She certainly didn't know what else to say.

"I'm Tyler. You're from London? That's so cool. What class do you have next?"

Surprised and more than a bit confused, Annie looked at her class schedule while her stomach performed back flips. Sure, she was tall, and some people said she looked kind of like a younger Kate Middleton, but gorgeous guys like Tyler didn't normally talk to her.

Still, she wasn't going to question it. "American History. Room 183."

"That's on my way. I'll take you there."

"Thank you." Was this really happening? Not only was this guy talking to her, he wanted to *keep* talking to her. She didn't know what it meant, but it had to be good.

"Do you like soccer?" Tyler asked. His smile was so dreamy Annie wished she could have a poster of him up on her bedroom wall. A floor-to-ceiling one.

Wait, he's stopped smiling. Oh, right. He's waiting for a response. What did he say?

"I don't play soccer, but I do like watching it," she said slowly, hoping that covered what he asked. It seemed to work; his smile returned.

"What do you think of Manchester United?" he asked.

Annie hesitated. Football rivalries ran long and deep. Opposing fans often got into arguments — sometimes even fights. What she said about Man U could determine whether Tyler kept talking to her or ran away. "I saw them play against Chelsea once. My dad took me."

Tyler stopped to look at her in awe. "No way! I've seen Chicago Fire play a couple times but that's nothing compared to what you have across the pond. I catch those games on TV sometimes, or online."

Annie smiled, glad Dad was more of a football than rugby fan. "It is nice to watch them live if you have the chance."

"Totally." He stopped outside a classroom and

jerked his head at the door. "This is you. See you around."

"Cheers — I mean thanks." She smiled back and stared at him as he walked away. She was really starting to like American high school.

"Out of my way." Kelsey knocked into her as she walked past.

Or maybe American high school was just as bad as she thought.

Chapter 3

Annie's knowledge of American history was limited to what she'd picked up from Dad and what she saw in movies. Somehow she didn't consider either source reliable. They were studying the American War of Independence, or the Revolutionary War as they called it over here. Annie knew almost nothing about it. There were other, much bigger wars to study in British history.

"Hope you Brits aren't still sore about losing," the teacher teased as he passed by Annie's desk. Annie kept her head down and focused on taking notes.

Before French class, Annie realized she really needed to use the bathroom. She had no idea where that was, though. There were a couple of friendly-looking girls talking next to some lockers. "Excuse me, could you tell me where the loo is, please?"

They looked at her as if she was from Mars. "The what?" one of the girls said.

Annie blushed. "Sorry. The ladies' room."

"Oh, sure," the other girl said. "Just around the corner on the left." But before Annie had even started in that direction, the girl turned to her friend. "Don't you love her accent? It's so cute."

Annie sighed. She wished people would stop

making such a fuss over her and the way she talked. At her old school, she had never stood out. She kind of liked it that way. Maybe Lexie could get her a button that said, "I've got an English accent. Get over it."

After French, Annie consulted her schedule again. Lunch. Brilliant. Half the day was done, and she was starving. Next time Dad made her a big breakfast, she was not leaving it untouched.

She found the cafeteria on her own, but it was full of people. Some of them had food, and some didn't. None of it really made any sense.

"Where do I queue up?" Annie asked a heavy girl with a green checkered shirt, biker boots, and short, spiked blondish-brownish hair.

"Queue up? I'm sorry, I don't understand," the girl said, looking puzzled.

"Where do I get my food?" Annie asked. "I'm new."

"Yeah, I kind of figured that," the girl said. She smiled and pointed. "Get in that line for food. There's another one for drinks, and a third one where you pay."

Pay, Annie thought. *Crumbs.*

Dad had given her some money for lunch. The paper money was easy enough to sort out with their numbers, even though they were all the same size and color. But the coins were a nightmare. Annie felt like she was dealing with play money when she looked at them. She couldn't understand why the five-cent coins were larger than the ten-cent ones. It made no sense.

Deciding where to sit was another question, but she wasn't stupid. She couldn't just ask someone where to sit.

She quickly noticed Kelsey at a center table with her ladies-in-waiting and some guys, including Tyler. Not that Annie was bold enough to have sat next to him anyway.

At another table sat a red-haired girl Annie recognized from English class — the one who'd asked the kilt question. She was with some cool but tough-looking girls who were showing off arm and hip bruises. Annie remembered how she used to compare injuries with her gymnastic friends. These girls must play the same sport.

With a sigh, she sat by herself at a far table. It was less intimidating than asking if she could sit with people she didn't know. Well, at least no one was noticing her now.

"You bought lunch? That's brave."

Annie looked up from her cheese sandwich and smiled when she saw Lexie. "I shouldn't have bothered. It tastes like cardboard and I don't think it's really cheese."

Lexie plunked down her tray. "It's not. Legally they have to call it 'cheese product' now. But whatever you do, stay away from the Sloppy Joes."

"That bad, huh?"

"If they're anything like the ones in middle school, they're edible, but they'll leave you in the bathroom for the rest of the day."

Annie cringed and set down her sandwich. "What are you eating?"

Lexie held up a plastic cup and grinned. "Ramen noodles. I'm practicing for when I'm a starving artist in New York."

"Is that your dream, then? To be an artist, I mean, not a starving person."

"Yup."

"Are you any good?"

In response, Lexie pulled a thick sketchbook from her bag and shoved it across the table. Annie flipped through the pages. There was a little of everything in the book, from caricatures with big heads to cornfields rustling in the wind and abstracts with geometric shapes.

Annie lingered on a family portrait that captured the Jones family personalities: Lexie, wild and individual; Mrs. Jones, preppy and perfect; and Mr. Jones, who Annie hadn't met yet, who seemed serious and intellectual judging by his glasses and tweed jacket. All of the sketches were really good.

"I like the comic strips the best," Annie said.

"Me too. They're the most fun. I'll probably join the manga club."

Annie took another tentative nibble of her sandwich. "Your abstracts remind me of things I've seen at the Tate Modern."

"You've been to the Tate?"

"Yeah, and most of the other museums. School trips, you know," Annie added quickly so it didn't sound like she was boasting.

Lexie stabbed her noodles and broth with a fork.

"I don't know how you left London. I'd give any-thing to go there. I mean Chicago is okay, the Art Institute is fabulous, but it's kind of far and there's nothing much besides cornfields between here and there."

Just then, there was a loud burst of static. A man's voice came over the sound system. "Hello, students. This is your principal. I just wanted to remind you that this Friday is our first pep rally."

Lexie covered her ears as the cafeteria exploded in a cheer.

"And if you like what you see there," the princi-pal went on, "please note that cheerleading tryouts will begin after class on Friday. Thank you and keep those brains in gear."

"Ha-ha." Lexie rolled her eyes. "Is it over?"

A pep rally. Just the sound of it was so American. Annie had no idea what to expect.

"I'll probably try out for cheerleading," she said casually.

Lexie looked at her as if she'd said she wanted to grow a second head. "Why?"

Annie shrugged. "Dad suggested it and I thought it'd be fun. I used to be quite good at gymnastics before I got too tall."

"I'm sure you'll be great at it. I just didn't think you were the cheerleading type, that's all," Lexie said.

"What's the cheerleading type?" Annie asked.

Lexie ran a hand through her wild hair. "You're right, I shouldn't be prejudiced. I'll tell you what — if you make the squad, I'll come to a game, just to cheer *you* on. Cool?"

Annie nodded. Lexie hadn't answered her question but she wasn't going to push it. It meant more that Lexie was willing to support her even if she didn't like it.

Maybe they really were becoming friends.

The rest of the day passed in a blur. Annie went to biology, PE, and technology, and suffered through a few more exclamations about her "cute" accent. When the final bell rang, Annie grabbed her books and raced over to Rosie Lee's.

She found Dad in the kitchen area, crouched

over next to the sink. He was wearing old jeans and had a wrench in his hand.

"I'm warning you," he said, shaking his wrench menacingly. "If you don't stop this instant, I'm going to rip you apart piece by piece."

"Talking to the mice, are you?" Annie asked.

Dad jumped and dropped the wrench on his foot. "Holy cow, Annie, you scared the bejesus out of me. What're you doing here?"

Annie dropped her bag and sat on the counter. "Let me have a think. I work for MI6 and I'm here to spy on you?" she said sarcastically. "It's after three, Dad. School's over for the day."

Dad looked at his watch and then held it up to his ear as if he didn't believe her. "Drat, the thing's stopped working again. Well, how was school? Learn anything?"

Only that American boys are massively hot (at least one in particular), Kelsey is still horrible, and the cafeteria food is close to deadly. "There are some differences, but it's still school. What about you? How was your day?"

Dad let out a melodramatic sigh. "Fine, except this faucet won't listen to me and keeps dripping."

Annie turned to the tap. Now that he mentioned

46

it, it was making a steady *drip-drip* rhythm. "Maybe you should call a plumber."

Dad crouched down and attacked the pipe under the sink. "Nonsense. I know what I'm doing."

Annie didn't say anything. She didn't have time. Dad had barely touched the pipe with his wrench when the pipe burst. Water sprayed everywhere as Dad tried to stop it with his hands. "Turn it off, turn it off!" he yelled.

Annie looked around, her arms held up to block the stream. "Where?"

"The valve. Out back. Hurry."

Annie raced out the back door. *Valve, valve, where are you,* she thought, searching wildly. Inside she could hear her dad swearing at the water, pipe, and everything in between. She finally found it, turned it one way, heard Dad scream louder, and turned it the other way.

Back in the café, Dad sat in a pool of water with his legs out in front of him like a rag doll. His hair was plastered to his face and water dripped down his cheeks.

Annie turned away. She bit her lip and covered her mouth. Her shoulders started to shake. She couldn't help it.

She let out the biggest belly laugh she had in a long time. Dad slapped the floor and pouted like a baby, but soon he too was laughing.

It took several minutes for them to calm down. Finally, Annie helped pull Dad to his feet.

Then she got out the mop.

"I think that's a sign to call it quits for the day," Dad said as he emptied the mop bucket.

"Good, because I'm starving." Annie placed a hand on her slim belly. "Tomorrow, I'm bringing my own lunch, even if it is babyish."

"Food? Now you're talking. What do you say we get pizza? Real Chicago style. Trust me, nothing else compares."

"What's so great about it?" Annie asked.

"For one thing, deep dish. For another, the sauce is on top."

"Really? Why?"

Dad thought about that for a bit. "I don't know

the historic reason but as a cook, I'd say it keeps the crust from getting soggy."

"Any kind of pizza sounds great right now."

"This kind is better than great," Dad said.

He ordered the pizza and they picked it up on the way home.

Dad didn't seem to mind being seen in his wet jeans. For the first time that day, people were noticing Dad instead of Annie. Dad, of course, loved the attention. After the second person gave him a funny look, he started strutting like the rappers on television.

"Da-aad," Annie said under her breath.

"If people are going to look, might as well give them something to look at." He jerked his head and gave a downward hand gesture to the old lady who stopped her shopping to stare at him. "'Sup?"

Annie grabbed his arm and moved him away quickly. She wouldn't put it past the lady to take a swing at him with her shopping bag. He didn't stop until they were a block away from home and there was no one around to appreciate his soggy rapper look.

At home, they polished off the pizza, by far the best Annie had ever had, and she headed up to her room to get started on her homework. She pulled out her new phone and looked at it. The only person besides Dad who had her number was Mum.

No calls.

It's the middle of the night in London, Annie reminded herself. But she wished Mum had remembered it had been her first day at school and had thought to call.

She finished her homework quickly — the teachers were obviously still easing them in after the long summer break. Then she turned on the computer. Maybe there was word from Georgie or Mel, her best friends at home.

In London, anyway. I guess this is home now.

Georgie and Mel had both emailed. But more importantly, there was an email from Mum.

Dear Annie,

I miss you already. The flat feels so empty without you. I just got in from the office. I've taken on a big case so it looks like I'll be doing even longer hours than usual. I hope your first day at school went well and that you found the lessons interesting. I ran into Nicola's mum yesterday and she sends their regards. I know that you must

miss your friends, but I'm sure you'll make new ones in
no time. Let's plan to Skype later this week; it feels like
such a long time since you left.

Love,
Mum xxx
P.S. Remember to keep your room tidy!

That was nice. Good to know she hadn't completely forgotten. But still, a call would have been
better. Things had been tense between them since
Annie had decided to live with Dad instead of her.
Hopefully, Mum wouldn't hold it against her forever.

Annie flopped on her bed, pushing the clothes
she rejected this morning onto the floor. A second
later she was up again. Remembering Mum's P.S.,
she picked the clothes up, folded them, and put
them in drawers.

Funny how Mum could still manage to nag,
even with an ocean between them!

Chapter 4

"Liberty Heights, are you ready to meet this year's very own Staaaaaags?" the announcer roared. The whole school cheered in response.

Well, not the whole school. Lexie doodled in her sketchbook while Annie clapped politely.

It was Friday, and the pep rally was in full swing in the gymnasium. Annie had survived a week at school, and it wasn't too bad; the classes were fine and she knew her way around now. She was still "that English girl with the cute accent," but there were worse things they could call her. Like "idiot," which is what Kelsey muttered every time they crossed paths.

"Put your hands together for the marching band and the cheeeeeerleaderrrrrrrrrs!"

The band struck up a catchy tune while three cheerleaders ran out and did a round off into two back handsprings.

Annie's brain clocked their gymnastics abilities without even realizing it. She and Lexie were at the top of the bleachers. From that distance, the cheerleaders' faces were a blur — but she was too preoccupied with their form anyway. After ten years of gymnastics, old habits died hard.

One of the brunettes bent her leg.

The other didn't stick the landing.

But that blond one was impressive.

"We're the Stags?" Annie asked, unable to take her eyes off the cheerleaders as the rest of the squad joined the first three in a blur of silver and blue uniforms.

Lexie nodded as she drew caricatures of the cheerleaders with devilish antlers.

The marching band was building up. Something was going to happen. Like a wave on either side, the girl cheerleaders fell into back bends as two of the guys walked on their hands down the middle. In a chain reaction, the girls kicked over and landed back on their feet. A second later the handstand guys flipped back to their feet. The crowd went wild. Annie could feel the adrenaline as if they were clapping for her.

"Why don't you like pep rallies? This is fun." Annie clapped and cheered with the rest of the audience. "We don't have anything like this back home. We Brits are much too reserved."

Lexie sighed. "It's all so egocentric. All this for sports, while the arts programs get cut all the time. And I'm positive that they don't have as many pep rallies for the girls' teams, even though last year the girls' basketball team won the regional championship."

Three different cheerleaders stood side by side, two climbed on top of them, and one more got on top to make a six-person pyramid.

"Who do we love?" they all shouted.

The audience screamed, "The Stags!"

The girl at the top of the pyramid fell back into the waiting arms of the guy cheerleaders, the two girls in the middle somersaulted forward and landed square on their feet, while the three at the bottom slid into splits.

Annie imagined herself in the pyramid. She'd probably be on the bottom because of her height. She could do great splits, but she'd rather be in the air. More thrilling.

As the band launched into the school's song, Annie turned back to Lexie. "It is unfair female athletes don't get the same attention. It's like that back home, too. I think gymnastics is one of the few sports where it's the opposite."

"It's just plain sexist. Do you know what our girls' teams are called?" Lexie asked, shading in her caricatures.

"Um, the Does?" Annie asked, thinking of the

name for a female deer. "That's the only thing that comes to mind."

Lexie snorted. "Nope. The Staggettes."

Annie scrunched up her nose. "That is a bit naff."

"I don't know what 'naff' means, but from the sound of it, I totally agree." Lexie turned a page in her book and began sketching the teachers with huge heads and big, dopey eyes.

The principal was on stage now. "Thank you, cheerleaders and band members," he said. The crowd quieted. "We have two games this weekend, so let's hear it for both the football and the soccer teams!"

The teams came running in from opposite ends of the gymnasium. The players stood in front grinning while the crowd cheered for them. Annie leaned on the edge of her seat, squinting to get a better look at one of the soccer players.

Was it him?

Yes, she was sure of it. That gorgeous run-your-hand-through-it hair and perfect body. No wonder he wanted to talk about the Premier League. Standing among the other soccer players, wearing the captain's armband, was Tyler.

He waved at the crowd and flashed such a dazzling smile that Annie was glad she was sitting; she might have fainted if she'd been standing up.

As the noise died down, the principal addressed the crowd again. But Annie didn't hear a word he said. All her attention was on Tyler, who was now chatting and laughing with the cheerleaders.

Well, that settled it. She was definitely trying out for cheerleading.

✼ ✱ ✼ ✩ ✼

After her classes finished, Annie raced to the locker room and quickly changed into a night-sky leotard and a pair of navy shorts. It had been a while since she'd worn a leotard, but it felt like a second skin to her.

Good thing I didn't give them all away, Annie thought. She pulled her long hair into a ponytail and was ready.

There were about thirty girls and two guys in the gym. Now, without all of the students there, the room felt incredibly big. Everyone kind of stood around looking at each other, not speaking, not knowing what to do, and not saying anything. If the idea was to make them sweat, it was working.

The door at the far end of the gym burst open and out came the cheerleaders in an intimidating group. This morning Annie had thought their outfits were nice. Now, the blue and silver sleeveless shirts and pleated skirts over blue shorts looked almost menacing.

Or maybe it was the fact that at the front of the pack, next to the coach, paraded Kelsey.

Of course. She was the one who had done the perfect round-off and back handsprings, and the two brown-haired girls next to her were her wannabes, also known as Bent Leg and Didn't Stick the Landing. During the pep rally, Annie had been paying too much attention to Kelsey's moves to notice her face. Seeing the expression on it now, Annie began to wonder if cheerleading was a good idea after all.

"As you know, I'm Kelsey, the captain," Kelsey spoke in a bossy voice that echoed across the whole gym. "We're going around with clipboards to get your details before we start."

Kelsey's eyes landed straight on Annie.

Oh please, let her go to someone else.

She didn't. She strutted right up to Annie and jutted out her hip. "This isn't roller derby, you know. Sure you're in the right place?"

Annie blinked. "Uh, yes?"

"Whatevs." Kelsey slapped the clipboard into Annie's chest. "Fill this out, but try to use normal spelling."

Annie wished she could think of some clever comeback that would make Kelsey back off. Nothing. Nothing clever anyway. She was at least pleased she was able to put, under experience, that she trained at the West London Gymnastics Centre.

And I'm not spelling it Center, Annie thought angrily.

Once they had everyone's details, Bent Leg (whose real name was Ginger) and Didn't Stick the Landing (Lulu) led the group in some warm-ups.

They started with jumps where you switched hands to tap the outside then inside of your heel and then the inside and outside of the other heel. It felt like Irish dancing with a lot more arm movements. Annie knew there were other ways to get the heart rate up without looking so silly and wondered if it was deliberate.

I wouldn't be surprised, she thought, looking at Kelsey.

Then they did some stretches, focusing on warming up their back, hips, shoulders, and abs. For thirty seconds they had to hold a straight plank as if they were about to do push ups. Easy-peasy. In gymnastics training they used to do one-arm planks. A couple of girls dropped to their knees, then quickly got back into the exercise when Kelsey glared their way.

Next they had to complete a circuit from one end of the gym to the other: three cartwheels on each side, straddle jumps, a backbend from standing, splits, and finally a sprint to the end of the wall.

Annie had no difficulties doing the circuit and felt fairly certain she did it well. The coach gave her the smallest nod, but Kelsey looked like Annie was giving off a bad smell.

Sigh. At least if I don't make it on the squad, I'll know why, she thought.

"Okay, gather around," Kelsey said. "I'm going to teach you a dance routine. Try to keep up, 'cause really, a baby should be able to do it." She scowled at Annie as she said it.

The dance was to an awful pop song that was just as popular in the UK as it was here. *Argh,* Annie thought. *Now this tune will stay in my head all day.*

Kelsey showed them the dance first before breaking it down. It seemed to involve quite a bit of hip thrusting and provocative gestures, or maybe that was just how Kelsey was doing it. When another girl joined her, the dance didn't seem quite so suggestive.

Annie decided to go with the other girl's style.

The steps weren't any more challenging than a floor routine and Annie caught on quickly, though some of the other girls found it hard.

One of the girls who struggled with the fitness part turned the wrong way, burst into tears at the sight of everyone glaring at her, and ran out of the gym.

Annie watched her leave, waiting for someone from the squad to go and comfort her.

No one did, and Annie wondered if she should. It was like survival of the fittest.

Just as Annie was beginning to imagine herself at the top of the pyramid, the hopefuls were taught the basic cheer.

"I want to see huge smiles on everyone and powerful projection from the diaphragm," the coach said. "Remember, cheerleading is ninety-nine percent attitude and presentation. If you're not perky and peppy, you're not doing your job."

This was the hardest part in the whole tryout: all the "rah-rah" stuff when Annie only wanted to work. Even her gymnastics trainer in London had tried to get her to smile more: "Think grace and serenity. No one wants to see the effort behind it." But Annie thought smiling felt fake, especially when she was working really hard.

That was something she'd have to get used to, being more outgoing.

More American.

More like Dad.

The coach clapped her hands. "Okay, that's it for today," she said. "Use the stuff you learned to come up with a routine for Monday for the actual tryout. Don't forget your enthusiasm and those smiles."

Annie forced her mouth into a smile and hoped it didn't look too much like she was in the dentist's chair.

Chapter 5

Tyler ran his hand through that irresistible hair and locked his intense green eyes on Annie's. "Hey, I scored some tickets for Saturday's game. Chicago versus Chelsea. Wanna go?"

Annie smiled. She had on her silver leotard under the blue and silver cheerleading miniskirt. She looked good and she knew Tyler thought so too. "Of course. But I'm supporting Chelsea."

Tyler took a step closer, his eyes never leaving hers. "I don't care, as long as I get to spend time with you."

"Good." Annie reached out a hand to pull him closer. She'd never made a move on a guy before, but this was no ordinary guy. Tyler was gorgeous and . . . fading.

"Stop!" Annie said. But he didn't. He kept fading until he was gone and Annie woke to find herself in bed, the sound of bowls clashing and the whirr of an electric mixer coming from the kitchen.

It was Saturday, so Annie didn't have school and she could stay in bed forever. Except the smells coming from the kitchen were too tantalizing to ignore.

Who needed sleep anyway? She knew she wouldn't be able to get back to the dream about Tyler.

In the kitchen, coffee was brewing, waffles were cooking, raspberries were on the table, and Dad was hand-whipping the cream. It was almost as good as any dream.

Getting asked out by Tyler would have been better, though.

"Am I the best dad, or what?" Dad asked. He tasted a bit of the cream with his finger. "Dang, that's good."

He slid a waffle onto a plate and placed it in front of Annie. Then he stood there, waiting, as she loaded it with raspberries and cream.

She took a tentative bite, frowning a little, just to make him sweat. The waffle was perfectly crisp. The cream was fresh. And the late-season raspberries from the local farmer were deliciously sweet. She couldn't lie; she wasn't as good at bluffing as Dad. "All right, I admit it. You are, undoubtedly, the best dad ever. These are fantastic."

Dad leaped into the air and punched it. "Aha! I knew it."

"But before it goes to your head, you'd better check the next waffle." Annie pointed to the iron, which was smoking. Dad rushed to take out his waffle, which was only slightly browner than ideal.

"So, what's the plan for today?" Annie asked once they'd finished their breakfast.

"I was hoping we could hang out with my other daughter," Dad said.

"Rosie Lee?"

Dad rolled his eyes exasperatedly. "She said something about a makeover. I don't know. I have trouble understanding what girls want these days."

Annie laughed. "I'll get my painting clothes on."

Rosie Lee's was really starting to come along. It no longer resembled a place where you'd likely get a side order of food poisoning. The former rodent tenants had been evicted and the display case mold hadn't returned to get its revenge.

Dad and Annie spent the morning and most of the afternoon painting the inside of the café an off-white that worked as a blank slate. The difference it made was huge: now it was fresh and clean and . . .

"Naked," Dad said.

Annie turned around to get the full view. "Yeah, it does feel like it's missing personality."

Dad nodded. "I'm not sure what theme I want. Something cool and hip. Maybe some black-and-white photographs of famous London landmarks? Or maybe a local artist would want to hang their work? Just as long as it doesn't look like my mom runs the café."

"Really? I thought some lace curtains would be nice at the windows and quaint tables with flowers and teapots covered in tea cosies . . ." Annie bit her lip and stared out of the window. It was the only way she wouldn't laugh.

Dad shook a finger at her. "No! Stop! This is a doily-free zone. I have to keep some manliness."

He backed up to check out the bigger picture. The paint tray was right behind him.

"Dad, watch out!" Annie said.

Too late.

He stepped in the paint tray and tripped over the bucket as he tried to straighten himself.

Globs of paint poured out even though he straightened up the bucket immediately. His sneaker was covered in paint and left footprints all over the floor.

Dad sighed. "That wasn't the look I was going for."

Annie laughed. "At least it has personality now. And it's definitely not Granny's style."

Dad made a face before he started laughing too. Together they cleaned it up, but there was still a stain embedded on the floor, and Dad's shoe remained covered in paint.

He scratched his head. "Now I have to figure out what to do with the floor."

A buzzing sound made them both jump and it took Annie a second to realize it was her phone.

Want to hang out?

Annie looked up. Dad was scratching his head as he stared at the paint stain on the floor. "Are we done here, Dad? Lexie just texted."

"Sure, go have fun. Leave me here all alone to clean up the mess." Dad threw his head back dramatically with his hand against his forehead.

"Do you really mind?"

"Of course not." Dad dropped the act and gave her a hug. "I'm glad you're making friends. See you later."

Annie had never been to Lexie's house, but she knew which one it was. A light-blue colonial with perfect white trimming, it made all the other houses look scruffy by comparison. Even the front garden was perfect. Not a single blade of grass seemed to be out of place. Lexie had said her mother took out a ruler to measure the grass's length. Seeing it up close, Annie thought that might actually be true.

When Lexie opened the door, Annie could see that the inside was no different: everything was perfectly arranged, as if it were staged for an interior decorating magazine shoot. It was so immaculate it was hard to believe anybody actually lived in the house.

Lexie's room, on the other hand, was completely lived in. Messy and artsy, it was exactly how Annie imagined it would look. One wall had a mural of a made-up world with pointy-eared people flying across the green sky and aliens fishing in the orange river. The other walls were covered with other artwork, posters of New York, and a mood board of the looks Lexie was going for that autumn. The desk and dresser were covered in clothes and accessories.

"I love all of your clothes," Annie said.

"Really?" Lexie replied, smiling. "You can borrow whatever you want. Mi closet es tu closet."

Annie helped herself to the clothes pile and put on a lime green tutu over her shorts and a pair of purple and pink legwarmers. She stood with her legs wide and crossed her arms in front of the mirror.

"You lookin' at me?" she said in a loud tough-guy voice to the mirror. The mirror was too scared to talk back, making Annie laugh at herself.

Lexie laughed too. "Wow, you actually look cool. Like a roller girl."

"Right." Annie turned from the mirror, her arms still crossed. "Everyone keeps mentioning that and I have no idea what it is. Is it some American slang?"

Lexie shook her head. "Better. Roller derby is a sport played on roller skates."

"Like hockey on wheels?" Annie asked.

"Kind of, but there's no ball or puck or whatever. Here, I'll show you. Easier than explaining."

Lexie turned on her computer and found some videos. They watched one with a pack of girls skating around in an oval and two other girls try-ing to break through them. One of the girls found a hole, snuck through, and the crowd went wild as she skated away on one leg.

"That looks wicked!" Annie exclaimed as they watched a video of one girl ducking through an opposing player's legs to score points.

"I know, right?" Lexie grinned. "And it's so much cooler live. Hey, check it. The Illinoisies are playing tonight in Prospect Park. That's not too far. Maybe we can get Mom to drive us."

"Think she will?" Annie asked.

"Sure, but let's make it sound like it's your idea."

They rushed down the stairs and found Mrs. Jones in the back garden tending to an immaculate flowerbed of red, blue, yellow, and pink flowers.

"Mom, do you think you could drive us to Prospect Park?" Lexie asked. "Annie wants to go to the roller girls bout there tonight, and I told her I'd go along if you could bring us."

Mrs. Jones set down her shovel. Even the silver blade gleamed under the rich dirt. "I suppose so. There's a house in Prospect Park I've been meaning to check up on."

"Yes!" Lexie spun in a circle like an excited dog.

"We'll go after dinner. Come down in about twenty minutes."

"Thanks," said Annie.

They dashed back up to Lexie's room. Right away, Lexie began flinging clothes in one direction and the other. "What to wear, what to wear?"

"I hadn't even thought about that," Annie said. She looked down at herself. She was still wearing her painting clothes, and while the tutu was fun, it wasn't really an option, no matter what Lexie said. "Can I borrow something? Do you have anything that would look good on me?"

"Bingo!" Lexie emerged with black-patterned tights and a pair of hot pants covered in gold sequins. She held them out in front of Annie. "Can you believe someone actually gave these away? They're tight on me, but should fit you just fine." She disappeared back into the pile of clothes.

"What should I wear with them?" Annie asked. Just then, a red top came flying in her direction. She caught it with one hand.

She pulled on the outfit Lexie picked for her and immediately felt like she was five and dressing up in her mum's clothes. Not that Mum ever had clothes like these in her wardrobe of smart business suits.

"I look like a tart," Annie said. She tugged at the hot pants, not that it helped. They were still insanely short. "I can't go out like this."

"Are you kidding? You have legs to the moon. You've got to show them off. How do I look?"

Annie turned to her. Lexie wore a black micro-mini, a pink off-the-shoulder shirt, and cream fishnets, which contrasted beautifully against Lexie's brown skin. She slid on a pair of large hoop earrings.

"Like we're both tarts."

Lexie laughed. "C'mon. That's the fun part. Derbies are great places to let your alter-ego show."

Lexie's alter-ego was obviously part punk, part gypsy. Annie relented. She was secretly impressed with her look. And even more impressed after Lexie applied extensive eye makeup. *I guess it's not like I'll see anyone I know!* she thought.

Mrs. Jones gasped when she saw how they looked. "Girls. You can't wear that in public. What about that cute corduroy skirt I bought you at the Gap, Lexie?"

Lexie rolled her eyes. "Ma, that's *so* not my style."

Mrs. Jones was about to argue, but then a man Annie assumed was Lexie's father walked in and put a hand on Mrs. Jones's shoulder. "Marilyn, let it go. She's a teenager." He added, "Lexie's discovering her own identity. Adolescents in every culture go through this process."

"You sound like an anthropology professor, Dad," Lexie said.

Mr. Jones smiled. "That's because I am."

"I suppose you're right," Mrs. Jones said. She sighed.

"Just this once," Mr. Jones said. He put an arm around his wife, which made her almost disappear into his chest.

"Guys, please." Lexie covered her face as if she was going to be sick. "Stop before I have to report you."

Annie thought it was great, though it gave her a bit of a pull in her stomach.

Lexie's dad was tall and African-American, the complete opposite of his petite, blond wife. Still, they seemed to complement each other perfectly. Mum and Dad were opposites too, but even before they separated, Annie couldn't remember a time they got along as well as Lexie's parents. She hated that her parents had split up. It made her feel split up too. But at least they weren't fighting now.

Chapter 6

After dinner, Mrs. Jones drove Lexie and Annie to Prospect Park. She dropped them off at the university's ice rink. "Do not talk to strangers," she said, "and call me immediately if you want me to pick you up early."

Lexie rolled her eyes. "Don't worry, Mom," she said. "We'll be safe."

Then they ran into the building. Rock music was blasting through the sound system and it was filled with families, college students, and what Mum called "alternative" types: green hair, tattoos, piercings, that kind of thing.

Maybe it was a good thing Lexie had dressed her up. Otherwise, Annie would have stood out for looking too "normal."

They paid for their tickets and searched for a place to sit. The ice rink had been thawed, and three taped ovals, one inside the other, marked the boundaries. Folding chairs were set up on three sides of the track, but the only seats left were the ones far at the back and the "suicide seats" on the floor.

"Is it safe?" Annie asked as they sat on the floor very close to the taped boundaries next to a sign that said Crash Zone.

Lexie shrugged. "Kind of. They skate in the

inner circle. If anyone comes your way, move — or you might end up with a roller girl in your lap!"

Annie felt someone looking at her. When she turned around, she saw the black-haired skater boy she met on her first day — the one with the dog named Sid Vicious. He gave her a thumbs-up as soon as their eyes met. She thought about heading over to say hi, but just then, the announcer started up.

"Gooooooood evening, ladies, gents, and all those in between. We have a great bout for you today. During the day, these ladies are moms, teachers, architects, herbalists, lawyers, you name it. But when they lace up those skates, they become the Corn Hustlers and our very own Illinoisieeeeeeeees!"

The crowd let out a loud cheer. Unlike at the pep rally, Lexie had no problem showing her enthusiasm as she stomped her feet on the rink floor. The announcer went on to introduce the women on each team. Most of their names were either sexy or vicious with puns intended like Viva La Diva or Psych O. Killya.

The women showed off their moves — and muscles — as they skated around the track in tights, short shorts, stripy socks, and yes, one was wearing a tutu. They knew they were hot and tough, but it was all tongue-in-cheek.

Four women from each team huddled up at the front and started skating when the ref blew his whistle. A few seconds later, two women further behind sprinted toward the group.

"Explain the rules to me," Annie said. Everything was happening so fast, it was hard to follow.

Lexie didn't look away from the women as she explained. "Basically, the two girls in the back with the stars on their helmets are the jammers. They're the ones who score. First they have to break through the pack — that's the rest of the girls. Then they skate fast around the rink to get behind the pack again and try to pass the members of the other team. Each opposing team member the jammer passes is worth one point. The other team is trying to block the jammer from scoring while helping their own jammer score points. They get penalties for pushing, elbowing, and things like that. If it's a major penalty, they get sent to the box."

Annie watched a few more rounds before asking her next question. "Why is that one girl, Bette Noir, flapping her arms at her hips?"

"She's the lead jammer, the one who broke free

from the pack first," Lexie said. "She can call off the jam whenever she likes. Usually to keep the other team from scoring or if she thinks she can't get more points. The lead jammer changes each jam, but Bette is the Illinoisies' star."

The bout was fast paced, full contact, and unlike any sport Annie had seen. Women got pushed, shoved, and knocked down all the time, but they'd get up and get right back in there. Sure, they swore and called each other rude names, but as soon as the whistle blew, they were laughing and helping up members of the other team. And best of all, they seemed to be having a great time.

By halftime, Annie was noticing holes in the pack where she would have squeezed through if she were a jammer. At one point, there was the most golden opportunity, if only the jammer, Poison Envy, had taken advantage of it. There was no one in front or behind one of her teammates who was bent low. The jammer could have easily vaulted over her teammate to score lots of points. At least if the jammer had been the imaginary Annie.

As the bout continued, Annie kept seeing herself in the jams. Jumping over the dog the other day when she ran into Kelsey was no fluke — she was a fairly good skater. But she'd never been in a position where other people were deliberately knocking into her.

It was a close bout, but the Illinoisies won 72-69. The crowd went wild when it ended.

While she and Lexie waited for Mrs. Jones to pick them up, Annie noticed some brochures on the merchandise table.

Fresh Meat Junior Roller Derby three-day workshop. Girls 14-18. All skill levels.

Mrs. Jones honked. Annie hesitated for a minute, then grabbed a brochure.

"C'mon, my mom hates to be kept waiting," Lexie said.

Annie folded the brochure in half and slipped it inside her top before running to the car. She was pretty sure Mrs. Jones in a bad mood would be even scarier than the roller girls she'd just watched!

Chapter 7

Cheerleading tryouts were happening after school, and Annie was having a hard time thinking about anything else.

It didn't help that Kelsey was obviously trying to psych her out. During lunch, she walked by with her two wannabes. "I don't know why we're even having a tryout," she said loudly. "We already know who we want. Obviously no one freakishly tall." Then, pretending that she'd just noticed Annie, her voice turned sweet as sugar. "Oh, hi, Amy. I didn't see you there. Good luck today. You're going to need it."

Annie slouched into her seat while Lexie shouted, "Her name's Annie, you dumbass."

Of course Kelsey knew her real name. Just like she knew Annie has been there listening to her. But was it true that they had already selected their new members?

"Am I really freakishly tall?" Annie asked the bacon sandwich she'd brought from home.

Lexie put an arm around her shoulders. Sitting side by side, it seemed as if they were the same height.

"You're not that tall," she assured Annie. "She was just trying to strike a nerve. She's just jealous of those supermodel legs of yours. You're so not a freak."

Annie sighed. "I guess. But maybe I shouldn't bother trying out."

Lexie shifted so that she could stare right at Annie. "Look, you know I don't like cheerleaders. But you can't let someone like that stop you from doing what you want. That's what *she* wants. She only said it because she knows you've got a good shot."

Lexie did have a point. Of the kids who had been at the first cheerleading tryout practice, Annie was definitely one of the top gymnasts. And her dancing wasn't half bad either. It was that perky, rah-rah, smile-until-your-lips-fell-off part that was her problem.

"You're right," Annie said. "I'm not going to let her scare me off. I just wish she wouldn't make me feel so nervous."

"I'll tell you my secret." Lexie looked around the cafeteria like cartoon characters do when they're trying to be inconspicuous. "In my head I draw a moustache on her every time I see her. The result is actually pretty good."

Annie laughed. Thank goodness for Lexie.

The locker room was like a ghost town. No one spoke or even acknowledged each other. All of the girls were too focused on getting ready in front of mirrors, curling or straightening their hair, and reapplying makeup. One girl was even stuffing what looked like chicken filets into her sports bra. When Annie sat down on the bench to change, the girl next to her moved her makeup bag away like she was afraid Annie would use it.

"I'm not going to touch it," Annie said. Everyone stopped what they were doing and stared at her for a few seconds, then returned their attention to whatever they were doing. Except for the girl next to Annie. She got up and sat somewhere else.

When they were ready, they filed out to the gymnasium and waited to be called forward. Annie hadn't expected to see so many people watching the tryouts. It seemed like half the school was there. She glanced around, wondering if there was anyone she recognized. Lexie had her manga club meeting, so

Annie knew she wouldn't be there. But she didn't expect to spot Tyler sitting with his friends on the second row.

Oh boy. Breathe, Annie, breathe.

He caught her staring at him and jerked his chin up in greeting. Annie raised her hand a bit and turned away shyly.

Crowds didn't usually make her nervous, but now that Annie knew that Tyler was there, her hands began to sweat.

"Listen up," the coach said in a voice that echoed throughout the gym. "You've got two minutes to show us what you've got in cheering, jumping, and dancing. I don't care if you do each element individually or one act that incorporates them all, just as long as you have a bit of all three in the two minutes. Quintana, you're first."

A girl with a high, dark-brown ponytail and too much makeup came forward with a perky smile. Her cheer was loud enough for everyone *outside* the gym to hear, and her dance moves were spot on. She didn't seem to have too much of a gymnastics background, but she could jump high and do cartwheels and backbends.

The next one was a guy who thought he was a

great breakdancer. Annie was sure head spinning was very hard, but the poor guy was so awful that it was more painful than impressive to watch.

"Turner," the coach called.

Deep breath.

Annie chose to do the cheer part first to get it over with quickly.

"Give me an S —"

"Louder," the coach yelled.

Annie tried to project more. Except her tongue just got muddled in her mouth. "Give me an S. Give me a, uh, T. Give me an S-T-A-J, I mean G, and S. What do you, uh, get? The Stags! Yay."

She pretended to wave pompoms in the air, because she'd forgotten to grab real ones, and slid into a split. She ended it with a terrified smile that showed all her teeth.

The crowd clapped politely, but Annie's attention was on Kelsey. Her face was set in a smug grin and she held out both her hands in the shape of a fat zero.

Annie's eyes narrowed and she shook her head slightly. *Sorry. You're not winning that easily.*

For the next part, Annie chose to modify a previous floor routine to show off her jumps and dance abilities. It was a high-energy number that displayed her flexibility, coordination, and ten years of gymnastics.

Hands-free cartwheels, 360-degree straddle jumps, fancy footwork, and the sassy attitude she hadn't managed in the cheer. She ended it with a series of back handsprings into a back tuck, which she landed perfectly.

Take that!

The crowd went wild. Tyler was on his feet, clapping his hands above his head, and he gave her a heart-stopping smile.

Annie walked back to the bench feeling like her legs were made out of jelly. The rest of the hopefuls stared at her with mouths agape. Annie almost felt sorry for the next girl, though she wouldn't have done her routine any differently.

Kelsey's smug smile had morphed into an ugly grimace and her stare was attempting to laser through Annie.

Annie shrugged and wore a real smile for the rest of the tryout.

Who cared what Kelsey thought? Annie had performed a great second part, and everyone, including the best-looking boy in school, knew it.

Annie was still feeling pleased with herself as she headed to Rosie Lee's after the tryouts. She just hoped her old floor routine was good enough to make up for the disastrous cheer.

If only they'd let her get away with just doing the tumbling and dancing parts of cheerleading and leave the "rah-rah" parts to the ones who were good at it.

And actually liked it.

She opened the door to the café to find Dad rushing around muttering, "Fire, fire!"

"What? Where?" Annie looked around in a panic and sniffed.

"No. Meant fire marshal. Must set appointment. Can't open." Dad ran around the kitchen looking up and down for something.

"What do you need?"

"Keys. Car keys."

Annie spotted the bunch of keys in the front pocket of his shirt and pointed. "Dad, there they are. It's okay. I'll go with you, help you sort it out."

Dad took the keys from his pocket and finally seemed to notice she was there. "No, there's nothing you can do, unless you can give me a brain transplant. I've got to get more organized if I ever want to get this place going. Thanks, though."

Dad kissed the top of her head as he headed out.

Typical Dad.

He could whip up the world's best crème brûlée, but filling out paperwork was beyond him. He'd already taken the Illinois Food and Sanitation Course, and passed with flying colors, as well as setting up the business licensing, but she wasn't surprised there was still more to do.

She just wished she could help him in some way. Do something that was sure to make Rosie Lee's a great success. She stared at the naked off-white walls and the raw floor with the paint stain still on it, and they stared back at her.

That was it!

Annie grabbed her phone from her bag and called Lexie.

"Hey, how did the cheer-weeding go?" Lexie asked. "I mean cheerleading."

Annie didn't want to think about that.

"First part was awful, second was pretty good.

But that's not why I called. Listen, how would you like to help me decorate Dad's café?"

"Decorate how?"

Annie paced around the café. Mum did the same thing when she was on the phone; it used to drive Dad crazy. Crazier, rather. "We painted it off-white over the weekend, and now there are two blank walls in need of some character. Maybe a mural like you did in your room or something? Any ideas?"

"I have a million ideas! But wait, are you serious?" Lexie asked.

"Of course. You should see the space. It needs an artist's touch."

"I'll bring sketches to school. Wow, okay, gotta go. Too many possibilities already. Bye!"

"Bye." Annie hung up and looked around the naked room. Dad was going to love her surprise.

Right?

Chapter 8

The next day after school, while she waited for Lexie, Annie watched Tyler and his teammates flirting with the cheerleaders. The confidence she'd felt the day before after her routine was gone. Even if she made the squad, there was no guarantee that Tyler would flirt with her. He was sixteen, a junior. From her few weeks at Liberty Heights, Annie already knew that juniors didn't usually hang out with lowly freshmen.

"Hey, ready?" Lexie asked, walking up to her.

Annie sighed and turned away from Tyler and the cheerleaders. "Is it true the cheerleaders don't cheer at the girls' games? That's what a girl on the soccer team was saying in French class."

"Yup," Lexie said. "Same as they don't get pep rallies."

"But why don't the cheerleaders cheer for them?" Annie asked.

Lexie shook her head. "If you're asking that, then maybe cheerleading isn't your thing."

Annie let it go. She kind of knew what Lexie meant. No matter how much people talked about equality and not discriminating, it still happened. Maybe if she made the squad, she could suggest they attend at least a couple of the girls' home games. She didn't see why not. From what she'd heard, the girls' teams were really good.

"I know something we'd both be into." From her backpack, Annie pulled out the junior roller derby brochure she took from the bout over the weekend and waved it in front of Lexie. "They have a three-day Fresh Meat workshop starting tonight. We should do it together."

Lexie laughed. "Me, a roller girl? Not in this lifetime."

"Aw, come on! Give it a try." Annie pressed her hands together and looked at her friend with sad eyes. "For me?"

"Stop it." Lexie held up a hand in front of her eyes. "Seriously, me and sports don't mix. I don't even know how to ride a bike. But you could totally rock it."

Annie sighed. She *was* going to try it, just to see what it was like. But it would be nice to have a friend there doing it with her.

When they got to Rosie Lee's, Dad wasn't there. "We're in luck," Annie said. "I don't want my dad to find out about this."

Lexie frowned. "Is he going to be cool with it?"

"Absolutely," Annie said, even though she wasn't

entirely sure. "Come on, I've been dying to see your ideas. Let's have a look."

Lexie pulled out her sketchbook so they could look through her ideas. One had black and white geometric figures. "That's cool," Annie said. "But it's kind of psychedelic. Not really what Rosie Lee's is all about."

"Okay," Lexie said. "How about this?" She flipped to a country landscape with quaint cottages and rolling hills. It was a great sketch, but not right for the café.

"I like it, but I'm not sure," Annie said.

Turning the next page, Annie knew she'd found it. "This one. It's perfect." It was a traditional red London double-decker bus filled with very realistic famous British characters and historical figures waving from the windows. Right away Annie recognized the Queen, James Bond, Mary Poppins, Shakespeare, Jane Austen, the Beatles, Robin Hood, Paddington Bear, Naomi Campbell, Simon Cowell, and Peter Pan, who was sitting on top of the bus instead of inside.

Looking at the bus and the "people" in it made Annie's stomach twist. She missed sitting on the upper deck and squealing with her friends that the driver was going to crash into the vehicle in front of them. And there was that time she and Dad pretended to be American tourists and asked the driver if he stopped at Hogwarts.

Annie distracted herself by pointing at a green figure in the middle of the bus. "Um, who — or what — is that?"

"The Loch Ness Monster!"

"Nessie on holiday in London? That's brilliant." Annie laughed.

Lexie grinned, very pleased with herself. "I'm glad you like it. This sketch was my favorite too. Woke me up at two in the morning; artistic brilliance has that tendency. So do bean tacos. Anyway, I'm going to go check my supplies and see what I need to get."

"Would you like some money?" Annie asked. "I don't know what paint costs, but I'd be glad to pay you back."

Lexie shook her head. "Are you kidding? This is like having a free art space. It's my dream."

Annie grinned. "All right then. I'll make sure you get a lifetime supply of scones once we're open."

"Deal."

After dinner, Dad drove Annie over to the roller rink in the old white pickup he'd bought off a friend. The building was more than a bit run down with the paint peeling and the roof looking like it had been patched more than once.

Most of the lights on the sign were burnt out, so instead of saying ROCKERS' ROLLER RINK, it read O K S   L   I K.

"Are you sure this is the right place?" Dad asked.

Annie didn't know. "That's what the brochure said," she said, but she didn't feel sure.

They walked in together, Annie with her roller-blades tucked under her arm. The rink was just as shabby on the inside as it was on the outside, with faded carpet and chipped plastic food tables. At the far end of the rink near the skate rental booth, some girls were getting ready.

A woman with long wavy auburn hair and a Celtic-style tattoo banded around her left bicep skated over the carpet toward them. "Hi," she said, holding out her hand to shake Annie's. "Susan Ritter. Are you here for the Fresh Meat workshop?"

Dad took a breath, straightened his shoulders, and ran a hand through his hair, which only made it stick straight up. "Yeah, about that. I'm not really sure if roller derby is the right fit for Annie. I don't want her to get hurt."

Annie was about to argue, but Coach Ritter beat her to it. "I completely understand — I have kids too. I'm not going to lie; girls do get hurt sometimes. But I'm a nurse and I make sure we keep a fully stocked first-aid kit onsite. No girl is allowed on the rink without proper pads, helmet, and a mouth guard. We take safety very seriously."

Coach Ritter smiled and Dad softened. "Great," he said. "Annie really wants to try it."

"I really, really do," Annie said.

Coach Ritter nodded. "Part of this Fresh Meat workshop is to get the girls familiar with safety and avoiding injuries, along with teaching the rules. We only use quad skates, though," she added, noticing Annie's Rollerblades. "So, Annie, why don't you get fitted into skates and pads, while your dad registers you and signs the waiver. You'll need to buy a mouth guard. We don't share those."

Annie thrust her Rollerblades into Dad's arms and headed to the skate rental booth before Dad could change his mind.

She stopped short when she saw the cute skater boy she met the first day. His shaggy black hair covered his light blue eyes, but he grinned when he saw Annie.

"Hey, I was hoping to see you here. Annie, right?" He pulled out some skates without waiting for Annie to say her size.

Annie blinked and looked down at the skates. They weren't pretty: brown and beaten up with lots of scratches, but they still seemed to be in great working condition. She sat down to try them on.

"That's right," she said. "Annie Turner. I'm sorry, I don't know your name."

He brushed the hair out of his eyes. "It's Jesse. How do those skates fit?"

Annie wiggled her toes and laced one up. "They're perfect."

Jesse shrugged even though he seemed quite pleased with himself. "I have a knack for anything with wheels. If you don't buy your own, I'll keep these tucked away for you."

"Thanks." Annie took the wrist, elbow, and

kneepads he held out. Blushing slightly, she looked down from his intense gaze and found herself leaning closer to him instead. She stared at his T-shirt, which had a black-and-white image of four guys with paper bags over their heads. "Is that The Damned?"

"Yeah, my Velvet Underground T-shirt was dirty." Then he looked up suddenly. "You actually know The Damned?"

Now it was Annie's turn to shrug. "Of course. 'New Rose' is a classic."

He looked at her as if she were a goddess. "I have *Damned, Damned, Damned* on vinyl."

"For real?" Annie gasped.

"Five bucks at a garage sale," Jesse said.

"I hate you," Annie said. She grinned.

"All right, peeps." Coach Ritter called, clapping her hands. "Let's get rolling."

Jesse held out a helmet. Annie put it on, buckled it, and stood up.

It was a little awkward to move in the quad skates. She hadn't been on that kind since she was a little kid.

Annie ran her tongue over her top teeth and remembered the guard Coach Ritter had mentioned.

Luckily Dad was still where she left him. In his hand was a white container. Annie skated over to him, opened it up, and popped in the blue mouth guard.

"All right there, Dad?" Annie asked. The words came out as if she had a potato in her mouth.

"What? Oh, yeah." He looked away from the skaters warming up in the rink and gave Annie a huge hug. "Be safe."

"I'll be fine. Don't worry," Annie said. He sighed and kissed the top of her helmet.

Annie watched him leave then turned her attention to the other skaters. Right away she noticed how different everyone looked. In gymnastics, all the girls were similar: short and compact. Here there seemed to be girls of all shapes, sizes, and builds. There was even one girl who was almost as tall as Annie.

"Hi, everyone, great to see so many of you," Coach Ritter said with a group of experienced skaters standing behind her, smiling encouragingly. Those roller girls didn't fit one image or mold either. Annie recognized a few from school, including the short red-headed girl who'd asked the kilt question in English class.

"This workshop is pretty much a skills training,"

Coach went on, "working today on agility and endurance. But really, it's about having a good time. Here to help out are some of the girls in the league. Liz, also known as ElizaDEATH, is a senior and on her fourth year of roller derby."

A tall blonde with broad shoulders and three piercings on each ear gave them two thumbs up.

"Holly Terror, one of our best jammers."

That was the girl from Annie's English class with the fire-engine-red dyed hair. Up close, she was the size of a ten-year-old, but Annie knew she was sixteen. She got onto her toe stops and posed like a model.

Coach Ritter introduced the others and then got down to business.

"We'll start with some stretches, really working on those hip flexors, before warming up. This will be a long and hard training, so make sure to drink lots of water."

The girls spread out on the rink and crouched down on their skates, straightening out one leg then switching to the other. A heavy girl with spiky blondish-brownish hair was stretching next to Annie.

"Hi, I'm Lauren. You asked me a question in the

cafeteria on the first day at school and I still feel bad that I didn't know what you said."

"Oh, hi!" Annie said. "Don't feel bad. Nobody understood me that day."

Lauren smiled. Her mouth guard had a leopard-print design. Annie grinned back at her.

They got up from their stretches and Coach Ritter got them to sprint around the track a couple of times in both directions.

The quad skates felt different from Annie's inline ones — her balance was a bit wonky — but even that didn't slow her down too much. She and Lauren were the only two to pass all the other girls before finishing their laps. Annie stretched her right leg out in front to stop. Nothing happened.

And then she crashed into the barrier.

Immediately, Liz was at her side. Annie hadn't fallen but the wind had been knocked out of her.

"Are you okay? You're trying to use your heel brake, except there isn't one on quad skates. Happens all the time. Just remember to drag your toe. Great laps, though." Liz gave her a friendly pat on the helmet and skated back to the rest.

After Annie caught her breath, they had to skate backward, twice in each direction. Here the quad skates did feel more awkward and it seemed harder to get a good flow. Other "Fresh Meats" were struggling with backward skating too, but Coach Ritter kept shouting out pointers while the girls in the league demonstrated proper technique. When they switched to the other direction, Annie thought about how she skated backward on the rollerblades and applied that same technique to push off. Much better. Smoother. With a bit of practice, she might catch up with Lauren.

As Coach Ritter set up some cones, Lauren skated up to Annie. "Isn't this great? You have no idea how long I've been waiting to be old enough to play. Now I don't have to take my brother's BS about not being able to play football."

Annie tilted her head to the side and then understood. American football, of course. "Do boys never play roller derby, then?"

"Not really. I think St. Louis is the closest men's team, but it's almost like a different sport; most of them don't have the you-know-whats to wear fishnets and pink bootie shorts."

Annie laughed and turned her attention to the coach.

"Great skating everyone. Now I'm going to have

you weave around these cones. I want to see you crouched low, back ends sticking out. That's the skater stance and I want everyone in that position all the time. You're down, you're grounded. You're up, you might as well be on the floor. Holly, why don't you show them?"

Holly skated toward them, spun around to change direction, kept skating backward, and then got on her toe stops right in front of them.

"So, you know those gross public bathrooms you really don't want to sit on? You want to get low enough so you don't pee on the seat, but not so close that you catch something vile."

There was a collective cringe from the girls as they imagined those public toilets. They watched Holly zip around the cones, crouched low, like it was the easiest thing. As they tried it out themselves, everyone shouted out suggestions and encouragement. Annie couldn't get over how supportive everyone was.

"That was good fun," Annie said when she skated back to Lauren.

"You're a natural. I bet you'll make the team."

"If anyone makes it, it'll be you. I barely know the rules or anything."

Holly had overheard them. "C'mon, guys," she said. "It takes more than one day to become a roller girl, and even then we're all still learning."

She had a point. Annie's gymnastics trainer had always said that if you thought you knew everything about something, you knew nothing.

Liz, perhaps inspired by Annie's crash, taught them how to stop. "The easiest way is to drag and press down on one of your toes," Liz said, demonstrating as she talked. "You can also do a snowplow, where you keep your legs wide and bring your toes together like a V. This is really, really useful when you're blocking in the pack. Makes you more solid. Just don't let your legs go too far apart or you'll end up doing a really painful splits."

The girls laughed at Liz's mock splits and her pained expression that seemed to be taken from experience.

Liz laughed with them as she straightened up. "If you feel more confident, you can try the T-stop," she continued. "One skate forward and the other behind it to make an upside-down T. The wheels on that back skate scrape against the ground to make you stop. But don't let the wheels touch the other skate or you'll wipe out."

"What about that one Holly does?" one of the girls asked. On cue, Holly skated over, turned backward, and skidded to a stop on her toes. A few girls clapped as Holly gave a little curtsy.

Liz nodded. "That's the tomahawk stop. Don't try it unless you're really good at switching from forward to backward. And try it slow the first few times."

They practiced the various stops. Annie mastered the basic toe drag and T-stop on both sides. She already knew how to do the snowplow because of skiing, but never felt it was a pretty stop. She practiced it anyway, just because Liz said it was useful. Then, with a deep breath, Annie tried Holly's flashy tomahawk stop. She barely had enough momentum to turn from forward to backward but she did it! Next time, she would up her speed from slug to turtle.

The last thing Coach Ritter had them do was play Red Light, Green Light. "It's simple," the coach said. "When I say 'green light,' you go, and when I say 'red light,' you stop. If you move without a green light, you go back to start. If you fall, pick yourself up and keep going. First one to cross the finish line wins. Okay, girls, places."

The girls crouched behind the line, one skate forward and hand on knee.

"Ready?" Coach Ritter called. "Green light!"

They dashed down for less than two seconds before Coach Ritter shouted, "Red light!"

Annie stopped using the T-stop she'd just learned and almost lost her balance. But almost wasn't the same as actually falling. With a few funky chicken moves, Annie managed to stay on her skates. Two other girls weren't that lucky and landed with a thump. But, laughing, they helped each other up before Coach Ritter shouted the next green light.

Halfway to the finish line and Annie was in the lead with Lauren right behind her. That's when Coach started getting playful. She got Lauren to return to the start with "green lettuce."

"And that's why I hate vegetables." Lauren skated back to the start but with a good-natured smile.

With every stop, Annie felt more confident and more in control of her skates.

"Green tomatoes," Coach Ritter yelled. "Green onions . . . green light!"

Annie sprinted a few good strides before having to dig in her toe to stop. The rest of the crowd was a good ten feet behind her.

Coach tried a different tactic. "I was driving the other day, saw a green car parked outside a green house. It was at a green light —"

Didn't work. As soon as she heard the word *light*, Annie was off.

Two feet from the finish, Coach Ritter yelled, "Red . . ."

Annie's gut told her to keep skating, and she was right: Coach followed it up with ". . . robin!"

Annie crossed the line and threw her arms in the air in victory. Everyone congratulated her, and some of them, including Lauren and Liz, gave her hugs. There were no sour grapes, no condescending fake smiles from anyone. Everyone was genuinely happy for her.

Annie unbuckled her helmet to wipe the sweat from her forehead.

That was brilliant, she thought. *Tiring, but oh so cool.*

She couldn't wait until the next practice.

Chapter 9

Before classes started the next day, Annie overheard two girls crying in the bathroom because they hadn't made the cheerleading callbacks.

"I checked the notice on the board like ten times. I can't believe they didn't want me," one of them sobbed into her hands.

"My life is totally ruined now," the other one wailed.

Callbacks?

The only "board" Annie knew of was the one next to the principal's office. Annie headed over there feeling a bit confused. Why hadn't anyone bothered to let her know the callbacks had been posted?

Unless she hadn't made it.

Or unless she had, and someone was hoping she wouldn't show up.

She ran her finger down the names. Had she made it? Yes! There she was: Annie Turner.

Her name was with nine other girls, no guys. Callbacks, this afternoon. Not only did she not know the list had been posted, no one had told her that the callbacks would be today after school.

And she had nothing with her to wear.

Dad could bring her something. He wouldn't

mind. After all, he was the one really pushing the whole cheerleading thing. Not that she was trying out for him; she had to see it through for herself. She wasn't a quitter.

She headed to her locker for the morning's books and found Lexie there. Today, she was wearing authentic bell-bottom jeans, a real tie-dyed shirt, and lots of homemade beaded jewelery. And a huge grin.

"I checked my supplies and we're set to paint that bus whenever," Lexie said.

Annie put the cheerleading callbacks out of her mind. "Brilliant. How about tonight? Dad's going out to play basketball so he won't be around to ask what we're doing."

"He still doesn't know?" Lexie asked.

Annie could just picture his smile when he saw it. Or at least she hoped he'd smile.

"I really want to surprise him. How long do you think it'll take?"

"Few hours, I bet. We might not have enough time to do it all today. Mom insists I get home by 8:30 on weekdays. She's convinced the predators start roaming the streets at 8:31."

"What if you spent the night?" Annie asked.

"Dad won't mind, my friends used to do it all the time in London."

"Let me ask."

While Lexie called her mom, Jesse came over. He pulled off his large DJ headphones and grinned. "Hey, Annie. How are you feeling after the Fresh Meat workshop?"

Annie rubbed her legs and moaned. "I'm aching all over. I'm sore in muscles on my back I didn't even know I had." She broke into a huge smile and added, "But I loved it. It was such fun, and the girls are really nice."

Jesse nodded as if Annie had just complimented his sisters. "Coach Ritter is awesome. She was a great jammer, Miss Demeanor, before a shoulder injury made her retire. The Illinoisies won most of their championships because of her. She'll make you work, but she really knows her stuff."

"She seemed amazing," Annie said.

Lexie got off the phone. "Mom said yes. Paint party!"

"Brilliant," Annie said, then explained to Jesse, "We're decorating my dad's café tonight."

"Sweet. What's the theme?"

Annie explained the bus to Jesse and turned

to Lexie. "Shall I call you when I've finished with callbacks?"

"You do know that callbacks are *this* afternoon, right?" a rude voice interrupted loudly. Kelsey stopped right in front of Annie with her two matching minions on either side.

No thanks to you, Annie thought. "Yes, I know."

"What callbacks?" Jesse asked.

"Cheer-weeding," Lexie muttered. Jesse crossed his arms and leaned against the lockers.

Kelsey ignored Annie's friends as if they didn't exist. "In case you actually make the squad, you should know you're not just a cheerleader during the games, you're a cheerleader *all* the time."

Annie frowned. "What do you mean?"

Kelsey sighed, as if she were explaining something simple to a toddler for the umpteenth time. Her minions rolled their eyes in unison.

"It means that cheerleaders represent the school," Kelsey said slowly. "People will expect you to *look* like a cheerleader, not some London freak." She raised her eyes as she glanced at Annie's outfit.

Unlike Kelsey, whose purple designer shirt and short suit looked like it came off the catwalk (her minions were sporting similar outfits), Annie was wearing her favorite Sex Pistols T-shirt and jeans. There was nothing designer about her clothes except that it was a genuine Sex Pistols T-shirt, and not some knockoff.

Jesse shifted his weight. He was just a little taller than Annie, but just as skinny, and not very intimidating. "Is that supposed to be an insult? Freak? Seriously, is that the best you can do?"

Lexie turned to him. "Brain waves are very painful for her."

Annie bit her lip. Laughing at the cheerleading captain might not be the best idea.

Kelsey pretended not to hear, though her voice was considerably louder as she continued to talk to Annie. "You should really think about who you hang out with, if you really want to be a cheerleader." Now Kelsey looked Jesse and Lexie up and down.

"Yeah, Annie. You really should think about it," Lexie said with a mock serious expression.

Kelsey ignored her. She just turned on her high heel with her minions behind her.

Jesse pushed his hair back and gave Annie a puzzled look. "You want to be a cheerleader? With her as captain?"

Annie tried to shrug it off, even though the look

on Jesse's face was the same as it would be if he'd discovered Annie was a flesh-eating alien.

Sure, Kelsey was rude and annoying, but that couldn't be true of all the cheerleaders. The pep rally had been fun, their uniform was really nice, and most of all, now that Annie started the try-outs, she wasn't going to quit. "I'm quite good at gymnastics."

"I never thought of you as the cheerleading type," Jesse said. "See you." He put on his head-phones and walked off.

Lexie sighed and raised her eyebrows at Annie. Annie sighed too. Her school in London had its cliques, of course, but she'd never felt that if she was a gymnast she couldn't be friends with someone from a different group.

Just because she wanted to be a cheerleader didn't mean she was going to start acting awful like Kelsey.

Annie had to borrow clothes from the lost and found to wear during callbacks. Dad was dealing with suppliers and wasn't able to bring her leotard to school for the tryout.

The options weren't too great. She settled for a pair of boys' long basketball shorts and a shirt she chose to wear inside out or it would have read "Hooters." It was the beginning of the school year, there was nothing else that fit.

Annie knew she had to make the most of it — there wasn't anything she could do about it. She wasn't Dad, who'd have a laugh while wearing odd clothes.

As soon as Annie walked into the gym, it struck her how everyone looked alike, both the cheerleaders and hopefuls. Of course there were racial differences, but everyone was slim and pretty. Just by being a little taller than the other girls, Annie felt like she stood out.

And the borrowed clothing didn't help.

Not that she wanted to look like them, but she wished there was more diversity in appearances.

Like in roller derby.

"Okay, girls," the coach said. "You're here because you stood out in the tryouts. Unfortunately, we only have room for four of you on the squad. So make sure to give it all you've got."

As soon as she said that, the girls stepped away from each other. Almost as if they were afraid the others would ruin their chances of making it by being too close.

Kelsey came up to them and burst out laughing when she saw Annie's outfit. "Looks like the circus is in town."

Annie looked down and felt her face flush. If only she could disappear, after taking a mighty swing at Kelsey.

I'm not going to let her get to me. I'm going to hit her where it hurts. By making it onto the squad.

Kelsey taught them a new dance routine to an even more disturbingly catchy pop song than the one she played the week before. With every movement Annie could feel the soreness in her muscles from yesterday's Fresh Meat workshop. Not that it bothered her. It was a nice reminder of a great night and how friendly everyone had been.

Today was different. There was no friendliness from anyone. It was every girl for herself.

One girl lost her balance during a turn and accidentally stepped on Kelsey's toes.

"You almost broke my foot, you cow!" Kelsey yelled. "I can't believe you. Only a total klutz would do that." She dramatically limped off to one side to sit down. Immediately Kelsey's second in commands hovered next to her.

The poor girl looked ready to burst into tears. Annie narrowed her eyes. She'd seen the misstep and really couldn't believe it hurt Kelsey that much.

If Kelsey were a roller girl, she would have laughed and helped the girl up, she thought.

"Watch where you're going, girls," the coach said. "And smile. Big, mouth-hurting smiles. If you're not hurting, you're not smiling enough."

Annie nodded. Then she spread her lips as far as they'd go.

She wanted to make the squad. But was that because she wanted to prove a point to Kelsey, or because she actually wanted to be a cheerleader?

Annie didn't know anymore.

Chapter 10

After callbacks, Lexie was waiting outside Rosie Lee's with a small overnight bag and another bag large enough to fit a body. "Art supplies," she said, gesturing at the bigger bag. "I had Dad drop me off. Can you imagine me hauling that the half-mile from my house to here?"

Annie laughed. "Not really."

She pulled out the keys Dad had given her and they both dragged the big bag into the café. Lexie looked around the space again and took a deep breath. "Are you sure your dad will like it?"

"Ninety-six percent sure," Annie said. "And if he doesn't, I'll paint over it."

Lexie whimpered at the thought, but smiled. "There are always lost masterpieces in every artist's life. Remind me to take a picture before we leave, just in case."

Annie switched on the old radio in the kitchen while Lexie sketched the outline of the bus. Even with just the faint lines on the wall, the café felt as if it were coming alive.

"That looks amazing," Annie said as Lexie started mixing paints.

"How good are your art skills?" Lexie asked, handing her a brush and a tray with red paint.

"I can paint within the lines. Is that good enough?" Annie said, her hand already itching to get started. Dad was going to love it. He had to.

"Perfect. The bus is all yours while I do the people. Once you're done, I'll touch it up a bit. Groovy?"

"Sure, Michelangelo," Annie teased. Then she smiled. Comparing Rosie Lee's to the Sistine Chapel might not be that much of a stretch once Lexie worked her magic.

"I like him. Wait, you're talking about the Ninja Turtle, right?" Lexie joked as she sketched out bus passengers. "Too bad there are no real famous British superheroes for the bus. I mean there's Captain Britain, I guess, but no one except comic-book nerds like me have heard of him."

Annie couldn't think of any either. Though that wasn't to say there weren't some cool British characters with special powers. "I'm glad you have David Tennant as Doctor Who."

"Of course. He's the hottest and he had Martha. I used to pretend I was her. Time and space travel would be so cool."

Annie nodded. "I don't fancy meeting some of those aliens, though."

"It's not like they'd be worse than the ones we already know." Lexie said.

Annie knew by Lexie's grin that she wasn't talking about green monsters from space with three eyes. "Which aliens do you mean?"

"The cheerleaders, of course," Lexie said. "I'm sure you figured out by now they're not human."

Annie laughed, but inside she was worried. Was she going to lose Jesse and Lexie as friends if she made the squad?

The next morning, Annie and Lexie burst into the kitchen, where Dad was having coffee and croissants still hot from the oven. "Dad!" Annie screamed. "Help!"

"What's the matter?" Dad asked, putting down his coffee.

"We overslept and you have to drive us to school, right now." Annie squeezed Lexie's hand, barely able to hold in her excitement.

Dad looked at his watch. "You still have plenty of time."

"No, we don't! The thing is, I left my school bag at Rosie Lee's, and there's this bit of homework I still need to do —" Annie stopped, afraid she was digging herself into a hole she couldn't get out of.

Dad got up from the chair. "Okay, calm down. Let me get the keys."

"And shoes," Annie reminded him.

"Shoes, snooze." But when Dad came back, he was wearing his sneakers, one of them still covered in paint.

Annie and Lexie each grabbed a couple of croissants before following him out to the truck. The girls squeezed in next to Dad in the front seat.

Dad sighed as he turned the key. "It's not like you to be so forgetful, Beanie. I think you've been hanging around me too much."

"No, it's just with school and cheerleading and roller derby and stuff, I forgot. Um, let's put on the radio!" Annie said, hoping to change the subject.

"Stuff?" Dad repeated. "Is that teen-speak for 'boy?'"

The girls burst out laughing. "So I'm right!" Dad said.

Annie sighed. There was no point in correcting him. He'd find out soon enough.

Dad parked the truck in front of the café. "I'll wait for you."

"No, I — uh — left my keys," Annie said. "Can you let us in?"

Dad frowned. "Next time, I might think twice about letting you have a sleepover on a weekday," he said. But he got out of the truck and walked up to the café.

He unlocked the door and turned on the lights. The whole café burst alive with the characters on the bus.

When they'd finished painting the night before, Annie had thought it looked good. Now, with the sunlight coming in through the front windows, the sight was spectacular. Every character on the bus was cartoony but instantly recognizable.

"Surprise!" Annie said.

Dad was speechless. He went up to the wall and touched Sherlock Holmes's face.

"Do you like it?" Annie asked. Suddenly, she was nervous. It didn't seem like a good sign that Dad was being quiet for a long time. That wasn't like him at all.

Dad's eyes were wide as he went from one person to the next, identifying them as he went along. "It's incredible," he said finally. "I love it. Who did this and how much do I owe them?"

Annie let out the breath she had been holding and grinned. "You don't owe anyone anything, except scones for life. It was all Lexie's idea."

"Not true," Lexie said. "Annie wanted to spice up the place. I just did the art."

Dad wrapped Annie in a big hug, and then pulled Lexie in too. "It's perfect, beautiful. Lexie, you are incredibly talented. You're like a modern-day Andy Warhol."

"I wish," Lexie said. She smiled. "Thanks."

Dad let go of them and went over to stare at the mural again. Then he turned back to them with a big frown. "I'm afraid there's a problem."

"What?" Annie asked. She and Lexie looked at each other nervously.

Dad crossed his arms and tapped his paint-covered sneaker. "You didn't sign it, Lexie. Art is worth nothing if it's not signed."

Lexie laughed and pulled a green marker from her bag to sign the right bottom corner with her full name: Alexis Raquel Jones.

Dad beamed. "Now it's perfect. And I'd better get you two to school before you really *are* late."

That morning, Annie felt like nothing would ruin her good mood. And after English class, it seemed like the day was only getting better.

After English class, Tyler came up to Annie's desk. He hadn't done that since the first day. Yes, he smiled and waved when they saw each other in the halls, but Annie assumed they were just "hi" friends. Not "coming over to her desk for a chat" friends.

"Hey." Tyler leaned over as she gathered her books. "Did you get that homework? Writing an essay on the current 'tone' of *Two Cities*. What does she want?"

Annie licked her lips. She knew what Ms. Schwartz meant, but how could she explain it? Especially when Tyler made her feel confused just by being around.

"Uh, I think we have to write about the mood so

far in the book. Is it happy, sad, sarcastic, that sort of thing."

Tyler nodded. "That sounds doable. Hey, how did the cheerleading callbacks work out?"

Annie blinked. He knew she'd been called back? Just the thought made butterflies do backflips in her stomach. "Not all bad."

"I love how you say that. 'Nawt ahl baahhd.' Your accent is really cute, you know?"

Instead of bothering her, like it did when everyone else pointed out her accent, Tyler's comment made Annie's insides flip-flop more. Did he really think her accent was cute? Was that his way of saying he thought *she* was cute? Or was he just trying to be nice?

"Well, American accents can be quite cute too," Annie said.

But before she could say anything else, Kelsey sashayed her way right between them. For once she was on her own.

"Tyler, did I tell you how great your penalty shot was over the weekend?" Kelsey said, linking her arm through Tyler's. "How did you do it?"

Tyler beamed and began to recap his goal. "Well, the first thing is to fake out the goalie," he said. He seemed to forget all about Annie as he and Kelsey walked out of the room.

But Kelsey didn't. She turned around and mouthed, "Mine," before laughing at whatever Tyler had said.

So much for the morning's good mood.

That night, as Annie worked on her English essay at the counter of Rosie Lee's, she came to a couple of conclusions: she had to be more assertive, and she had to start going to soccer games at school. It was the only way she would have a chance with Tyler.

"M'lady, might I interrupt?" Dad said in an old-fashioned accent.

Annie saved the document and closed her laptop. The essay was done, and she could double-check it before class tomorrow just to be sure.

"If you must." Annie straightened herself and pretended she was the mistress of a grand estate.

Dad bowed. "M'lady, might I offer you a sample of this year's harvest?"

"That depends. Of what harvest do you speak?" Lady Anne peered upon the manservant with distaste.

The manservant revealed a tray from behind his back and placed it in front of Lady Anne. "If it pleases, m'lady, I have before me a new-fangled meal brought to my attention by the Earl of Sandwich himself."

Lady Anne peered at the mounds of bread suspiciously. "And what, pray tell, are in these concoctions?"

"Only the finest, choosiest ingredients for m'lady." The manservant pointed to each mini sandwich individually. "Tender ham and Dutch gouda cheese laced with apple sauce. Shaved turkey and fresh mozzarella with pesto and tomato. And finally, roasted mushrooms with chèvre from the local dairy and avocado imported from the land of California."

Lady Anne waved her hand in distaste. "That shan't do. I will only consume avocados from the land of Florida. You know that. Now take them away immediately."

"Very good, m'lady." The manservant bobbed his head and picked up the tray to head back to the kitchen.

"Oh, bring it back, you." Annie dropped her act. "I thought you were going to serve British food: shepherd's pie, bangers and mash, roast beef and Yorkshire pudding, things like that."

Dad set the tray back on the counter. "I figured it'd be best to start with pastries and sandwiches, which I can make ahead of time, and see how it goes. If I do hot meals, I'll have to hire someone. I've tried to be in two places at once. Doesn't work." Dad sighed.

"That makes sense," Annie said, picking up the first sandwich. "But your Yorkshire pudding is my absolute favorite." She took a bite. "Yum!" she said. "Delicious."

"So you really think people will buy them?" Dad stuffed his hands into his apron to hide how nervous he was.

"Dad, Rosie Lee's is going to be a hit. I know it." Annie started in on the next sandwich.

Dad hugged her and planted a kiss on the top of her head. "You're a great daughter."

"I'm just being honest."

"I know. That's what makes you so great. Let's go. It's almost derby time."

At the rink, Jesse seemed happy to see Annie when she got her skates, but he didn't say much. Her skates were ready and waiting on the counter when she walked in, but Jesse just nodded when she thanked him. *He's probably reserving judgment about me until he sees what I'm like as a cheerleader,* Annie thought.

Annie and Lauren were the first ones to put on all their gear and start warming up with figure eights. Once everyone else was ready, Coach Ritter waved them all to the center of the rink. "All right, gather round for a sec." She waited while the girls skated toward her. "First of all, I'm so glad to see you; we've had a few girls decide not to come back and I wish them well. Today, we're mainly going to work on blocking. This is a contact sport, so everyone needs to know how to block. If you can't block, you can't be a jammer. Simple as that. To get you ready for that, you'll need to know how to push your way through the pack." She narrowed her eyes. "Now, how many of you like shopping?"

About half the girls raised their hands. "Well, we're doing a different kind of shopping today," Coach Ritter said, "with a drill called Shopping Carts. Get into groups of four and choose who's going to push the cart first."

Annie was put in the group with Liz and two girls whose names Annie had forgotten. The one with glasses said she wanted to go first.

"Now line up, single file," Coach Ritter said. "Hold on to the hips of the girl in front. Whoever's at the back has to push the line of girls to the other end of the rink. I want everyone crouched real low, knees bent, booties out. Ready . . . go!"

At first, Annie thought it was kind of fun having someone else making her go. But then as the girl in the back went faster, it was harder for her to control the "cart" and make sure they went in a straight line. Not that that made it less fun. At one point, they did a complete 360-degree turn that made everyone burst into laughter.

When it was Annie's turn, she realized that three

people on wheels was a heavy amount to push. The game was fun and everyone enjoyed the craziness. Getting on her toe stops helped to get the other girls moving. She could feel the effort in her thighs and bum as she leaned and pushed them toward the finish line.

Coach Ritter clapped as the final group pushed their "shopping cart" to the designated area. "Good job, everyone," she said. "Keep in mind you can use a variant of that in an actual jam. Your own team-mates can be props. You can grab her by the hips or grip her arm to whip around the pack. That's totally legal. You can even roll over her back if the opportunity is there. Just don't knock her down or use the other team as a prop. All right. Now."

A few girls let out scared chuckles. Annie sympathized; she knew what was coming next.

Blocking. Oh joy.

When she saw the Illinoisies play, Annie had imagined herself as a jammer. She was fast, agile, and lean. Blocking might just break her. But if she couldn't block, she'd never become a jammer.

"We're covering booty-blocking today. This is your biggest blocking asset, if you get what I'm saying." Coach Ritter patted her own backside. "Keep looking over your shoulders — you want to know where the jammers are all the time. Stay low, like we've been practicing." She clapped her hands. "In pairs, one girl is going to booty-block the other, who's trying to get around her. I don't want to see any grabbing or elbow blocking."

Lauren was first and paired up with Mattie, one of the girls in the league. Lauren seemed to know exactly what to do and really set the standard for blocking. Her size helped, but she was also quick and let her hips swing back and forth as she skated from one side to the other. Her head snapped from one shoulder to look over the other, never caught off-guard.

"Yeah, Lauren!" Liz cheered, and everyone else joined in to cheer her on. One girl, Aiko, whistled loudly. Annie clapped until her hands hurt.

When it was time for Lauren and Mattie to switch roles, Lauren didn't allow the experienced girl to pass her once. Annie was sure Lauren would make the team.

Three more pairs went before it was Annie's turn. She was paired up with Holly.

"Pass or block first?" Holly asked.

From what Annie had seen, neither seemed like

something she could do. "Uh, pass please," Annie whispered.

Annie crouched down, feeling like a giant next to an ant. But maybe that was a good thing. Holly was tiny. She couldn't be too hard to pass.

Right?

Wrong.

Annie was vaguely aware of people cheering and the coach shouting suggestions, but she couldn't really hear them.

Holly was right in front of her, and every time Annie tried to get around her, Holly swung her hips around to keep her from passing.

Think assertive. See a gap and go for it. Fake her out.

Annie sprinted to the side, changed directions, and then immediately changed back to the original side. For the smallest second, she thought she had made it.

But no. Holly wasn't fooled.

Changing the angle of her skates, she cut across the track and was at Annie's side in an instant. With a big swing of her hips, she made contact with Annie's side.

Annie's skates left the ground. Not just her skates, all of her. She was in the air, flying. She reached out, trying to grab onto something . . . anything . . .

And then she landed on her back with a loud *thump*.

Chapter 11

"Are you crazy?"

Annie blinked. It took a second for her eyes to focus, and a few more to understand what she was seeing.

She was on the floor of the rink, staring at a ceiling fan going around and around. Holly was at her side. Also on the ground.

It was a few more seconds before Annie realized Holly was the one talking.

If you could call it that.

It was really more like yelling.

"Never, ever grab another girl and bring her down! Never!" Holly screamed. "Grabbing like that can cause a pile-up and get you kicked out of the bout."

"I'm so sorry," Annie said. "Are you okay?" She eased herself up to sitting, feeling a bit light-headed. Thank goodness for helmets.

"No, but I'll live." Holly skated off, not showing any signs of an injury other than a face that matched her fire-engine hair.

Coach Ritter dashed to Annie's side and dropped to her knees.

"Annie, honey, look in my eyes," Coach Ritter said. "Can you move?"

Annie stared at the coach's green eyes. She was still a little dazed. One minute, she had been about to zip past Holly, and the next they were both on the ground. "I think so."

Coach Ritter checked her over, paying special attention to her spine and head. Her back was hurt and her elbows were really sore even though the pads had taken the brunt of the fall. At least everything seemed to still work. When the coach finished the examination, she jerked her head to one of the girls. "Liz, help me get her off the rink."

Liz rushed over to help. Both Liz and Coach Ritter kept their arms around her as they skated off. Annie could feel the spot where Holly had blocked her on the thigh. It would bruise for sure. Despite being so small, Holly could certainly hit hard.

All of the other girls were watching. Annie started feeling self-conscious with all the attention she was getting. Holly had fallen too, and no one was helping her off the rink.

Liz and Coach Ritter led Annie to a bench and skated back onto the rink. Immediately, Jesse was next to her with a bottle of cold orange juice. "That was some wipe-out," he said, giving her a look that was half concern and half respect.

"That floor is really, really hard." Annie drank her juice as she watched the rest of the girls going through their blocking.

"The first major fall is always the worst. But now you're initiated as a real roller girl. Every fall will just make you better. Build character." Jesse pointed to the faint scar above his right eye. "Once, I wiped out on a half-pipe. The board tip hit me square in the head."

"That's awful."

Jesse grinned. "Six stitches."

Annie finished her juice and stood up. She was glad that she and Jesse were cool again — it seemed like he'd forgotten that she might turn into a stuck-up cheerleader. But she hated all the attention she was getting.

The girls kept glancing over at her with worried looks, and twice Lauren had mouthed, "Are you okay?"

It was like they didn't think she was tough enough to handle a fall.

"I'm going back," she said. "Thanks for the juice."

She threw the bottle into the recycling and skated back onto the rink. Her hip and thigh ached every time she used that leg, her back felt like it had been slapped by a giant hand, and her elbows would have broken if she hadn't been wearing pads, but none of it was serious. Nothing to keep her from continuing on with the training. No one could call Annie Turner a quitter.

Coach Ritter nodded her approval when she saw Annie back in the group.

"Now's probably a good time to cover falling," the coach said. "If you've taken martial arts, you probably learned to tuck and roll. That's fine as long as you don't roll into anyone. Remember to 'fall small.' That rule keeps you and the others safe. What I'm going to teach you is to fall forward whenever possible. That's where your pads are. That's where you're most protected."

She had Liz and Holly demonstrate a block and a fall. Holly blocked and Liz faked a fall, landing squarely on her hands and knees. A second later, Liz was back on her skates.

"That's your four-point fall. You can also aim to land on your elbows or forearms," Coach Ritter said. "Whenever you fall, get up as soon as you can and keep skating."

That's where I went wrong. That's why they were

fussing over me. I just sat there like a weakling instead of getting up.

Next time, Annie knew, things were going to be different. Now that she knew what to expect, she wouldn't be so dazed.

Liz blocked Holly this time and Holly dropped to one knee, got back up, and fell on the other knee. She made the move look so graceful, it reminded Annie of figure skaters.

Two other girls, Sam and Keisha, demonstrated the baseball slide. "Since you're landing at an angle, instead of straight on the leg," Sam said, "it doesn't hurt."

"That much," Keisha added. Both girls laughed, but Annie cringed.

The last fall was a simple double knee drop that Coach Ritter called the "rock star" fall. From her knees, Holly brought her toe stops under her and used them to get herself up and off down the rink.

Once all the falls had been demonstrated, Coach Ritter set up cones in each corner and had the Fresh Meat skate around the rink performing a different fall in each corner.

"Get comfortable with the falls," she called out as they skated. "Don't be afraid of them. Now is *not* a time to communicate — don't announce you're falling. If someone falls in front of you, it's your responsibility to avoid her. You need to be prepared to clear any obstacles in your way."

Annie tried all the falls a few times. While they skated, Holly made a big show of staying clear of Annie. Annie sighed. She wished that Coach Ritter had shown them how to fall before she'd taught them to block.

Annie found the four-point the most efficient but the one-knee was still the prettiest. Annie wanted to spend more time perfecting it. The baseball slide wasn't too bad after all, but she didn't dare try it on her sore side. That could wait for another day.

The best part was that now that she knew how to fall, she wouldn't bring anyone down with her again. She didn't need any more enemies.

When they had finished the falling drills, most of the girls were panting, but everyone seemed to be pretty pleased with themselves.

"Great job, everyone. I'm really proud." Coach Ritter looked at them each in turn. "You've all come really far. Tomorrow, I'll be giving you a skills test to see how much you've learned. It's not a competition, and I hate making you do it, but the fact is that if you can't perform these skills, it's not safe for you to play. However, if you sign up for more training and keep practicing, I'll welcome anyone, anytime you pass. In my book, roller derby is about accepting, not selecting. Stretch and cool down."

As soon as Annie took off her skates and pads, she lifted her shorts to check out the bruise on her thigh. It was already about four inches wide and more than a little purple. Just brushing against it as she shifted her shorts was painful.

"Ooh, that's a beauty." Lauren peered at Annie's bruise. "You should ice it once you get home."

Annie eased her shorts back in place with a moan. "Good idea."

"Derby isn't for the prim and proper, Princess Kate," Holly said as she walked by with her equipment bag.

Annie pressed her lips together. It wasn't the first time someone had said she looked a bit like Kate Middleton, but this time it sounded like an insult. "Kate is actually a duchess," she shot back. But as soon as the words left her mouth, she realized how silly and childish she sounded.

Holly scowled. "Who cares? This is a hard-core sport. If you can't hack it, don't bother."

Annie wasn't complaining about her sore spots. No one could say they'd heard her complaining. If anything, she was admiring the damage. The last time she'd had such a big bruise was when she missed her footing after a tuck and landed sideways on the balance beam.

Just because she was English didn't mean she wasn't tough. And tomorrow during the skills test, she'd prove it.

Lauren gave her a friendly punch on the shoulder. "You did great." Then she high-fived the roller girls as if she were already part of the team and swaggered out of the building.

The roller girls talked and laughed with each other as they headed out.

Annie's stomach tightened.

They belonged. They were all part of a group. Last time Annie felt like that was at the West London Gymnastics Centre.

Oh God, how she missed her friends. Nicola, Georgie, and Mel.

It seemed like such a long time ago — such a long time since she fit in *and* was part of a group of friends.

Back at home with an ice pack on her leg, Annie fired up the computer. Maybe one of her friends had emailed her. Maybe there was some news or mention of how much they missed her.

No. But there was an email from Mum.

Annie, I'm working all night on this case. If you get a chance, Skype me so we can have a chat. Miss you!
Mum

Annie opened Skype. Before she could do anything, the computer was flashing and ringing with a call from Philippa Bradley.

Annie gulped.

Bradley. Mum had gone back to her maiden name. It made the separation seem final.

"Hi, Mum." Annie pulled on her headphones. Through the wall that separated her room from Dad's, she could hear him snoring already.

"Annie, sweetheart, how are you?" Mum adjusted the camera so she was centered on the screen.

Her shoulder-length, light-brown hair had been re-dyed a darker shade since the last time they'd talked.

"Fine, tired." Annie shifted the ice pack, glad her mum couldn't see what she was doing. "Your hair looks nice, Mum."

Mum's blue eyes narrowed. "What's wrong? Is your father running you ragged getting that silly café ready?"

"No, nothing like that. It's just —" Annie paused. She didn't usually talk to her mother about these things. She talked to Dad. But Dad was asleep, so she went on.

"It's just that I miss you, I miss all my friends. I miss good tea. I miss being in a place I know."

"Oh, sweetheart, I'm sorry. I miss you too. Did something happen?" Mum asked.

"No, not really," Annie said. She sighed. "It's just that I'm trying out to be a cheerleader, but my friends don't like cheerleaders, just because the captain is a bit of a pain."

"It's always difficult when friends don't get along," Mum said kindly. "But ultimately, if they don't like you just for being a cheerleader, then they're not really your friends."

Annie knew Mum was right, but she didn't want

to think about that. She liked Lexie and Jesse a lot already. "Yes, I know."

"And what about that rollerskating thing you were telling me about?"

Annie straightened up, feeling the stiffness from landing on her back. Even so, a huge grin spread across her face. "It's so much fun, and the girls are brilliant." *Except maybe Holly*, she thought. "But I still feel like an outsider."

Mum nodded, pushing her glasses up her nose. "You know, you can come back here. I can make all the arrangements, talk to your headmistress, won't be any trouble at all. What do you think?"

Annie didn't know what to think. She was only saying how she felt — she hadn't meant that she wanted to go back.

Did she?

She shifted the ice pack again and stretched out her elbows. Even if she didn't get onto the roller derby team, she'd miss the friends she had already made.

She scratched a bit of red paint off her finger left from the mural at the café. She would really miss Lexie. And Rosie Lee's grand opening.

And Dad.

She couldn't leave Dad.

On cue, Dad gave a loud snore through the wall and then was silent.

Annie smiled. "Thanks, Mum, but I'll stay here for now. I'm not ready to give up on America just yet."

Besides, Annie thought with a pang of sadness, *it's not like I'm still part of my gymnastics group. I'd feel like an outsider in London too.*

Mum sighed and suddenly seemed very tired. "Well, give it a think and let me know if you change your mind. I really miss you and would love to have you back here with me."

"Thanks, Mum. I miss you too."

"I'd better let you go. If I finish this paperwork soon, I might get two hours of sleep."

"Don't work too hard. Love you," Annie said.

Mum blew a kiss at the screen. "I love you too, sweetheart."

The window closed, and Annie let out a big breath.

What would it be like living with Mum? It wouldn't be that bad, would it? Look how much Mum wanted her back. It could work. Maybe.

Or maybe not.

They hadn't gotten along that well when Annie lived in London. Annie knew half of the reason they were getting along so well now was because they were living thousands of miles apart.

But that didn't make her miss her mother less.

Chapter 12

The next morning after her shower, Annie wrapped a towel around herself and headed to her room to get dressed for school.

Dad passed her in the hall and gasped. "Annie Turner, what is that on your leg?"

Annie twisted around and noticed a giant black and blue bruise. She shrugged it off. "I'm fine. It barely hurts anymore."

Dad crossed his arms. "Right, and I married Pinocchio's mother."

"Dad, I —"

"Don't 'Dad' me. This is serious. I really don't think this roller derby thing is a good idea. That is a nasty bruise. Do you have more like that one?"

Annie hugged the towel tighter around her. He couldn't make her give up derby. He couldn't.

"I'm fine, really. And I know how to fall now so it probably won't happen again. Jesse says the first fall is always the worst."

"The first fall?" Dad repeated. "You mean it happens a lot?"

Annie bit her lip. The sport was played on roller skates and a big part involved blocking each other. There were bound to be falls. And many of them. "It's not as bad as it sounds."

Dad paced around in a circle, pulling his hair straight up like an arch over his head. Then he sighed. "Don't you find out about cheerleading today? That seems less dangerous."

He obviously hadn't met Kelsey.

"I honestly don't know if I'll make it. The head cheerleader thinks I'm a freak."

Dad narrowed his eyes, and then laughed when he realized Annie was serious. "The squad would be crazy not to have you. Now, go get dressed before that puddle gets any bigger."

Annie put on a black shirt and a denim skirt over black tights, a step up from her usual jeans and T-shirt. She wanted to look nicer in case she made the cheerleading squad, but the clothes still worked for roller derby later that afternoon.

It was the final day of the Fresh Meat workshop, and the day of the skills test. Annie had no idea what to expect. Even if she didn't pass, she hoped Dad would let her sign up for more practices. She wasn't ready to give up on derby.

Annie and Lexie walked to school together. Lexie was trying to figure out how to add Alice in Wonderland to the mural at Rosie Lee's. "She's a classic, but there's no more room for her on the bus and it would make Peter Pan less hilarious if he has someone riding on top with him."

"Maybe you can have Alice waiting for the bus?" Annie suggested.

Lexie nodded. "I'll think about that. And it's not just Alice. I should also have put in Frodo or Bilbo Baggins. I don't know how I forgot a hobbit. And Mom said I have to have Churchill."

Annie put an arm around her and gave her a squeeze. "It's perfect the way it is. Honestly."

"Thanks," Lexie said, smiling. "That's the problem with being an artist, you never think it's done."

They got to their lockers just in time to hear the principal begin the morning announcements. "Good morning, students. First of all, I have a very special, confidential envelope that was handed to me by the cheerleading coach. After a grueling tryout, as some of you know, may I present to you your new Stag cheerleaders."

Annie grabbed Lexie's hand. This was it.

"Dani Quintana!"

Annie and Lexie heard a loud scream from the homeroom next to them.

"Tiffany Lu!" Annie remembered her; she always had a huge smile.

"Maggie Mae McLaughlin!"

Annie let go of Lexie's hand. She hadn't made it. Kelsey just had too much power. That cheer part was rubbish. And maybe she just wasn't as good a gymnast as she thought.

"And Annie Turner!"

What? No way!

"Congratulations. Please confirm your acceptance with the captain by Monday. Make us proud," the principal said and turned off the PA system. The bell rang and they headed to their first class.

"This is a first. Me, friends with a cheerleader. I don't know if I can handle it," Lexie said with a grin.

Annie gave her a quick hug. "Remember, first game, you've got to be there. You promised."

Lexie rolled her eyes. "Yeah, all right. Just as long as it doesn't interfere with manga. Or my pottery classes. Or painting my nails."

Annie pushed her playfully. "Oh shut it, you."

"Fine, I'll be there," Lexie said. "But I hope you won't be offended if I bring my sketchbook."

"I insist," Annie said. "But no drawing me with devil antlers."

"You see how you are? Five minutes as a cheerleader and you already think you're better than the rest of us." Lexie winked. Then she headed off to first period.

Annie knew she was kidding. But what if being a cheerleader *did* change her? It wasn't impossible. She already felt different from the Annie she had been back in London. Not worse, just different.

When she got to English, Annie sat at her usual desk and opened her notebook. "Hey, I heard the big news," Tyler said, sitting down at the desk next to her. "That's so cool you're a cheerleader!"

Annie blinked in surprise. Usually he sat toward the back with his friends — and Kelsey. Not that Annie was complaining about the new seating arrangements.

"Thanks." She could feel her face turning red and hoped it wasn't too noticeable.

"It's going to be great having you cheer at my games," Tyler went on. "Too bad we're playing away tomorrow. But next weekend, you'll be there. It'll be awesome."

Awesome. Yeah, having an excuse to stare at

Tyler would be awesome. *If only I could actually speak*, Annie thought. *That might be even more awesome.* There he was, sitting right next to her, and she could barely open her mouth.

"Yeah." That was it. All she could say.

At least Ms. Schwartz walked in then, starting the class and cutting their "conversation" short.

Try as she might, Annie didn't hear much of what Ms. Schwartz said. She was too aware of Tyler right next to her. So close. If he wanted, he could reach out and touch her.

At one point, she casually let her hand drop to her side so it was there if he wanted to hold it. Then she brought it back to the desk immediately, blushing even more.

How stupid can I be? she thought. He wasn't going to hold her hand. Especially not in the middle of a class. He probably didn't even like her like that. He probably had a girlfriend.

It was probably Kelsey.

Annie took her time to gather her books at the end of class, hoping Tyler would disappear before she made a fool out of herself. She thought Tyler would walk out with his friends, but he lingered as she got her things together.

And then Kelsey sashayed her way over to Annie's desk. "Hi!" she squealed, giving Annie a quick hug that made her want to cringe and disinfect her clothes. "I'm SOOO glad you made the squad."

Annie glanced from Tyler, who was beaming, to Kelsey, who was showing enough teeth to rival a crocodile. What was she trying to do?

"Um, thank you?" Annie said.

Kelsey linked her arm through Annie's and led her to her next class — and away from Tyler. As they walked down the hallway together, Kelsey gave little waves at the people who turned and looked at them. She kept up her crocodile smile as she said, "As you saw with the tryouts, very few have what it takes to be a cheerleader. I mean really, practices Mondays, Tuesdays, and Thursdays, sometimes two games per weekend? It's a huge time commitment."

"Yes, I know," Annie said. She tried to remove her arm from Kelsey's grip, but Kelsey held on.

"I just want to remind you what an *honor* it is to be a cheerleader," Kelsey said. "It also means you're popular, so don't do anything that will bring the rest of us down."

Like being mean to the new girl? Annie thought bitterly.

Kelsey finally dropped her arm with a conde-scending pat and headed away. "Bye!"

Thanks for the welcome to the team, Annie thought. *Good to know I can trust you.*

Kelsey was right about one thing. Cheerleaders were popular. Practically every person — student or teacher — who passed Annie in the halls congratu-lated her on making the squad. Even the janitor gave her a thumbs-up.

It wasn't that Annie wasn't pleased to make the squad. She was. She just didn't want to brag about it to everyone at school.

A whole day of Kelsey's fake smiles and every-one congratulating her was too much for Annie. Roller derby practice couldn't come soon enough.

The day before, her skates had been on the counter, waiting for her when she got to the rink. Today they were nowhere in sight and Jesse was leaning against the rack with his arms crossed.

"You're here," he said, sounding surprised.

Annie frowned. "Yes. Why wouldn't I be?"

"I don't know. Derby kind of takes over your life." Jesse shifted his weight from one side to the other.

"Is that a bad thing?"

"I just thought that now you're a cheerleader, you'd stop slumming it with us."

Annie sighed. Couldn't he see she was still the same person? "Are you kidding? Being here is the highlight of my day."

Jesse relaxed and pulled out her skates. "For real? I figured we'd lost you to the dark side."

Annie pulled her laces up tightly and strapped on her pads. "Well, maybe I'm just what the cheerleading squad needs. A bit of light." Then she put on her helmet and joined the rest of the Fresh Meat.

Their warm-up drill today was a game of leapfrog. The girls crouched low and, one at a time, they used each other's backs to push off with their hands to jump over the "frogs."

Annie remembered playing leapfrog when she was younger. But with skates, it was a whole new game.

She leaped like she was supposed to over the first

few girls, but they were crouched so low, it barely counted. Except the last person. Lauren.

When she saw it was Annie's turn, she raised herself to about three feet off the ground and gave Annie a challenging grin. Annie couldn't resist. She knew she could do it.

Annie skated toward her, placed her hands squarely on Lauren's back and leaped over with her legs dangling on either side. She landed on all eight wheels, did a 180-degree turn, and stopped on her toes.

"Awesome." Lauren gave her a high five before they both crouched to the ground for the next frog to leap over them. Looking over at Liz, who stood a few feet away, Annie could tell that the older girl was impressed.

Coach Ritter clapped her hands once they'd all had a chance to pretend to be leaping frogs. "I hate this part," she said, "but it's time for you to show me what you've got. Like I said yesterday, this is for safety reasons only. If you've got the skills, you're in the league. While you're waiting your turn, Holly will lead you in some conditioning. Aiko, you're up first."

Holly waved them to the middle of the rink

where the refs skated during bouts. By the way Holly avoided being close to her, Annie knew she was still mad about yesterday's knock down.

While they waited for their turns at the skills test, Holly got them to do leg rotations at the hip, crunches, and girly push-ups on their knees. Annie tried to keep her attention on what she was doing instead of looking at the girls on the track, but it was hard.

At one point, she caught a glimpse of Lauren weaving through a minefield of cones. Lauren would definitely make the team.

"Annie, you're next," Coach Ritter called. Annie took a deep breath and skated to her and Liz. "First I want you to skate around three times at the fastest speed you feel comfortable, making sure you don't go out of bounds. After the third lap, stop any way you like. Ready?"

No, but she was going to do it anyway. Annie nodded. Then she got low.

Coach blew the whistle and Annie pushed off with her toe to sprint away. She rounded the corners with leg-over-leg crossovers, feeling like she could fly. After the last turn, she dashed to the end as if there were a finish line. With one skate behind her body, she dragged the wheels to a perfect T-stop. Liz nodded and made some marks on her clipboard.

Next, Annie had to jump over a few lines taped on the rink, side step in both directions, do two kinds of falls, go through the cone minefield like Lauren had, and then skate backward and stop. Backward skating was still a challenge, but at least she was improving. The last thing she had to do was booty-block one of the other newbies, a girl named Jordan with small black braids and a huge smile.

Blocking made Annie the most nervous of all the tasks being tested, but it also made her the most determined to do her best. She managed to keep Jordan from passing her, but only because the other girl was as inexperienced as Annie. Then she was done, and all that was left was to wait for the results.

When everyone had completed the test, Holly led all the Fresh Meat in a game of Simon Says while Liz and Coach Ritter compared notes and declared the verdict. Annie could feel her hands sweating as they played. *At least it's not cheerleading*, she thought. *They're not going to make me wait very long.*

"All righty," Coach Ritter said. "Here are your new roller girls, in no particular order. Lauren, Aiko, Annie —"

She went on, but Annie let out a scream and didn't hear the rest of the names. Lauren grabbed her in a huge hug, and soon, six other girls joined them. Even the girls who didn't make it were good sports and congratulated the girls who had.

Annie did a little happy dance on her skates that the others quickly tried to copy, resulting in a lot of arms flinging about and one girl on the floor, laughing. Annie couldn't wait to tell her parents.

"Good job, everyone," Coach Ritter said. She and the older roller girls clapped. "If you didn't make it, come talk to me and I'll give you some feedback on what you need to work on." She added, "If you made it, practices are here Mondays and Thursdays with bouts on the weekends. You need to attend practice to skate. See you next week."

Annie gasped. Mondays and Thursdays? No.

No way.

Annie put her head in her hands. Cheerleading practices were Mondays, Tuesdays, and Thursdays. She couldn't be in two places at once. She'd have to choose. But which one?

The one she was better at, or the one she liked better?

Chapter 13

"Hey, Annie, check this out." Dad took the cast-iron frying pan off the heat. With a little shake first, he flipped the pancake high into the air. It did three flips before he caught it in the center of the pan. "This pancake is a better gymnast than you, Beanie."

Annie raised her eyebrows and reached out for the pan. "Let me try."

Dad let out a huge sigh. "I suppose. Nice and easy. Just a flick."

Annie jiggled the pan like Dad had and flipped the pancake in the air. It flipped once and landed half in the pan. The other half broke off and landed on the gas flame. Dad grabbed the half pancake with his bare hands and flung it into the sink.

"And that's why, kids, you don't try this at home." Dad pretended to be stern but he was amused. So was Annie. Last time she'd tried to flip a pancake, all of it had landed on the floor.

A loud knock came from the front door. Annie opened it to find Lexie standing there with a midriff-baring black and white shirt, high-waisted pants with suspenders, and saddle shoes. A white beret perched on top of her unruly hair. She sniffed the air. "Wow, it smells even better inside."

Dad poked his head out of the kitchen to grin at Lexie, then turned to Annie. "Miss Turner, shame on you. Go offer the young lady a seat. I still have to finish up the flapjacks."

"Hungry?" Annie asked.

Lexie peeked into the kitchen and grinned. "I can eat. If there's enough."

Dad snorted. "As if that's even a question," he said.

Annie set the kitchen table for three and gestured to Lexie to sit. Then she brought out a teapot of hot water, a jug of milk, and a basket of tea bags: black, green, and herbal.

She stood back and kept her hands behind her. "And what would you like to compliment your pancakes, miss? Lemon and icing sugar?"

"Butter and maple syrup, if you have it?" Lexie asked, playing along with the game.

"Of course." Annie nodded and turned to Dad. "Order in. Short stack, fat and sweet." In movies, the American cafés always had code names for the food. She wasn't sure if what she said made sense but it sounded good to her.

A few minutes later, Dad set down four plates. Three held three pancakes each — one with butter and real maple syrup in little sauce cups, one with lemon slices and dusted with powdered sugar, and one with the works. The other plate was piled high with thick bacon.

"Wow," Lexie said to Dad as she took a bite. "If you want another daughter, I can offer myself up for adoption."

"Of course," Dad said. He steepled his fingers together and gave them an evil grin. "I can always use another indentured servant for the kitchens. I figure twenty years should cover your debt."

Lexie waved a hand at him. "No problem. Though once you get *my* decorating bill . . ."

Dad narrowed his eyes and growled before the three of them burst out laughing. They clinked their cups of tea and chowed down. Annie couldn't help but wonder if this was what it was like to have a sister.

"So what's the verdict on cheer-weeding versus derby?" Lexie asked, dipping a piece of bacon into the syrup.

Annie sighed. "I don't know. I really wish I could do both."

Lexie nodded. "But you can't. Not unless you split yourself in two. Or clone yourself, I guess."

Annie pushed her playfully but couldn't help imagining what it'd be like to have a clone. *One of us could go back to London and the other could stay here with Dad.*

"Well, I think you should go for cheerleading," said Dad. "Less chances of getting hurt. String beans aren't as good with bruises."

"Yeah," Annie agreed. To the bruises, not the cheerleading. She still didn't know about that. The pep rally had been so great, and having the whole school watch her perform at the next one would be nerve-wrenchingly brilliant. But she liked the idea of competing more than cheering along the side-lines. And there was no doubt that the girls on the derby team were much nicer. And real.

"Just think," Lexie said. She gave Annie a wide cheerleader's smile. "If you're a cheerleader, you'll be like one of the most popular girls in like the whole universe!"

"All righty. Girl talk is always a sign to bail." Dad pushed himself away from the table and stacked the plates on the kitchen counter. "Gotta get some more supplies. I have a challenge for you. See if you can come up with a new recipe — cookie, cake, anything you like — that we can sell at Rosie Lee's."

Annie and Lexie looked at each other. A challenge involving baking? Bring it.

They put the dishes in the dishwasher and cleaned up the kitchen. "Why are we cleaning first?" Lexie asked.

"One of Dad's few rules," Annie explained. "He always says to make as big of a mess as you need to while you're baking, but never start with a dirty kitchen." She gave the counter a quick swipe with a towel, and then clapped her hands. "What should we make?"

Lexie's eyes widened. "How about some kind of cupcakes?"

"Ooh, yeah. What kind?"

"Chocolate is always good."

She was right, of course, but Annie wanted to try something different. Something that the people of Liberty Heights had never tasted. She swirled the last bit of the tea in her cup.

"Hey!" she said. "What about Earl Grey cupcakes?"

Lexie frowned and sniffed one of the tea bags. "Orange?"

"Close," Annie said pulling her hair into a ponytail. "It's called bergamot. I think it's Mediterranean."

"Cool, let's try it. Mind if I plug in some tunes? I brought my MP3 player and dock."

Lexie didn't wait for an answer. In just a few seconds, Billy Idol's song "Rebel Yell" was pumping throughout Rosie Lee's.

"Nice!" Annie gave her a thumbs-up before taking the eggs out of the fridge.

"I'm so glad you dig classic rock," Lexie said. "Most kids at school just listen to the mainstream stuff: pop, rap, and hip-hop. No imagination."

Annie remembered the annoying pop songs they had to dance to during the cheerleading tryout. If she joined the squad, there'd be no getting away. "Yeah, I've noticed," she said. "Boring. That's all the cheerleaders like."

Lexie seemed to understand what she was saying. Or not saying. "They really like their Top 40," she said.

Annie started measuring the ingredients. On her seventh birthday Dad had shown her how to make her own cupcakes and she'd never forgotten. The only thing that would be different was to reduce the amount of milk a little to compensate for the extracted tea. She might not be a whizz in the kitchen like Dad, but she knew her way around.

"I still don't get why you want to be a cheer-leader. I mean, is it just to be popular like Kelsey?" Lexie asked as she lined the muffin tin with colored paper cups.

"Kelsey is a you-know-what. I don't want to be anything like her. It's just that . . ." Annie stopped. She shouldn't have said so much. "I don't want to give up on gymnastics."

Lexie squinted at her. "Really? Gymnastics? That's the only reason?"

"Well." Annie brushed away a stray strand of hair that had come undone from her ponytail. "There is another reason, but it's embarrassing."

"You're dying to show off those insanely long legs in that sickeningly cute uniform?"

Annie laughed. The uniform was cute, but no. She took a deep breath. Nicola, Georgie, and Mel back at home knew about him, but that was differ-ent. They weren't here. She might as well tell Lexie too. She was her best friend now.

"I really fancy Tyler," she admitted. "You know from the football — I mean, from the soccer team. I just thought if I was a cheerleader . . ."

"He'd get to know you better?" Lexie finished for her.

"Pretty stupid, huh?"

Lexie didn't say anything for a bit, and it wasn't just because the electric mixer was so loud. "Look, I don't know him well, since he's a junior and all, but I've heard he's kind of a player. I don't want you getting hurt."

"He seems really nice." Annie remembered the talks they'd had: Chelsea Football Club and her accent. He cheered so loudly during her tryout, he had to at least like her as a friend.

And then she remembered him flirting with the pretty cheerleaders during the pep rally.

"But it doesn't matter," she said quickly. "He's way out of my league."

But oh, how great it'd be if they did end up going out. Before taking a penalty shot, he'd look over to the sidelines, catch her eye and signal, "This one's for you, babe," before scoring the goal that would win the game. Then she'd run into his arms —

"Chief, we have a problem," Lexie said to a pretend walkie-talkie. "Girl, fourteen, British accent, seems to be suffering from delusions."

Annie pressed pause on her daydream and sighed. Lexie was right. Now was not the time. Tyler fantasies could wait, the cupcakes couldn't.

They put the pans in the oven and started to think about the icing.

"What about lavender? Think that will go well with the berga-thingy?" Lexie read the flavors Dad had in stock while Annie sang along with Siouxsie and the Banshees' "Jigsaw Feeling."

"Why not?" Annie swung her ponytail around in headbanging mode, and then jumped when her phone vibrated in her pocket. "Hold on," she said. "It's probably my dad."

No, it was a number Annie didn't recognize. "Hello?" she said as Lexie lowered the music.

A familiar voice responded. "Why haven't you confirmed your spot on the squad? I thought it was very clear that everyone, even you, has to formally accept."

"Kelsey?" Annie asked nervously.

"No, the Easter Bunny," Kelsey said, her voice so loud that Lexie heard, making her stick out her teeth — and chest — and hop around like a cheer-leading rabbit. Annie had to turn away to keep from bursting out laughing.

"Oh, right," Annie said into the phone. "Sorry about that."

"So? Are you confirming?"

Annie stared out of the lacy curtains Dad still hadn't removed from the kitchen. "Um, can't I let you know on Monday?" she asked.

Kelsey made an exasperated sound. "You mean you actually have to think about it? People would kill to be on the squad."

"It's just —" Annie started.

But Kelsey cut her off. "Whatevs. Just remember practice is Monday. And please tell me you're not actually listening to that crap I hear. So uncool." And she hung up before Annie could defend the Dead Kennedys.

"Boy, aren't cheerleaders, like, sooooo sweet and nice?" Lexie asked in the same mocking voice she had used before.

"Shut it," Annie said with a grin. If she became a cheerleader, she'd have to deal with Kelsey *all* the time. How did her minions manage it?

She shook her head and tried to push Kelsey out of her mind.

They took out the cupcakes and breathed deeply. The smell was heavenly.

When Lexie wasn't looking, Annie pinched off a tiny piece to taste it still warm. Dad always scolded her for doing that, even though he did it too.

They waited for the cupcakes to cool before adding the icing (which Annie also sneaked a taste of). "You're the artist," Annie said, pushing the bowl toward Lexie. "You frost them."

"You got it," Lexie said, wielding a small spatula. She sculpted and shaped the icing of each cupcake into a beautiful form.

There was no point in Annie helping her. She put the kettle on instead — you couldn't have Earl Grey cupcakes without Earl Grey tea to compliment them — and tidied up the kitchen. Once they were both done, the two sat down with a cup of tea and cupcake each. The result? Bliss.

Annie put her cup down and started on a second cupcake. "It's a shame good tea is so expensive here. That is the one thing I miss the most about London."

"What, more than your mom?" Lexie asked.

Annie sighed. "No, of course not. It's just . . ." How could she explain her mother to Lexie without making her sound uncaring? "My mum is really work-driven," she said, choosing her words carefully. "Some nights she wouldn't even come home until two in the morning."

"That's really late," Lexie said.

Annie nodded. "And she expected the same thing from me and gymnastics. Nothing but the best. I trained with the top coaches in London. She kept saying that I was going to be the next Nadia Comaneci — she was the first gymnast to score a perfect ten."

Annie licked the icing slowly off her cupcake. "But when I couldn't compete anymore, I think Mum took it worse than I did. If I couldn't be the best gymnast, then I had to be the best something else, but there's nothing else I'm anywhere near as good at. I still don't think she understands me. I love my mum, I really do, but she's nothing like Dad."

Lexie peeled away the paper from her second cupcake. "My mom doesn't get me either. I mean, she's okay with my art, but I know she keeps hoping it'll be something I grow out of."

"At least she's not putting pressure on you. Your mum is really nice. It must be great having her around all the time."

Lexie sighed. "Except when she starts nagging me about not being popular. 'When I was your age, everyone knew me and I always had a boyfriend. I don't understand why you don't.' Of course, she was a cheerleader."

Annie laughed at Lexie's perfect imitation of Mrs. Jones. "Maybe we should swap mums like they did on that show."

"Yes! Can I go to London? Like today?"

Instead of continuing the game, Annie let out the sad truth. "She's probably working. Today, and tomorrow, and every day."

Lexie gave her a big hug. "She's probably working more now because she misses you so much."

Just then, Annie's phone buzzed in her pocket. It was a number she didn't recognize.

come down to the skatepark. a bunch of us are chillin. - Jesse

How did he get my number? Annie wondered. Then she remembered that Coach Ritter had passed out contact details at the end of the last session. Jesse was a non-skating official, so he got the list too.

Before Annie could respond, there was another text. This one was from Lauren.

Bring your skates and some munchies to the park. Picnic on wheels!

As she was reading it, a text from Liz came in:

Some of us are hanging out at the St. Augustine Park on Dalton Street if you want to come.

"Looks like we have some options for the afternoon," Annie said.

"I don't want to hang out with cheerleaders," Lexie said. "Except you."

Annie laughed. "Better than cheerleaders. Skate park. Let's pack up the cupcakes, save a couple for Dad, and head down there."

Lexie jumped to her feet. "Now *that* I can handle. Skater boys are hot."

It took the girls half an hour to walk to the skatepark on the outskirts of town. Annie had never been there before, but knew right away she'd be hanging out there again. There were half-pipes and rails, stairs and a flat track. Every person who owned wheels, whether skateboard, roller skates, bicycle, and even one boy in a wheelchair, seemed to be taking advantage of the lasting warm weather to show off their tricks.

Liz, Lauren, and a couple of other girls who played roller derby were practicing blocking. Holly was using the track like a figure skater and showing off her jumps to the roller hockey boys.

Lexie placed herself at the picnic table with her sketchbook to guard the food. Jesse's dog, Sid Vicious, sampled a few of the cupcakes, paper wrappers and all, as soon as they had put them down.

At Jesse's insistence, Annie climbed the ladder leading up to the half-pipe and laced up her rollerblades. It looked a lot steeper from up above than it did from the ground. Almost a sheer drop. Maybe the half-pipe wasn't such a good idea.

"If you die," Lexie called out, "I'm moving into your house."

Annie stuck her tongue out and then grinned as she buckled a borrowed helmet. "Why wait? We have a spare room."

Before she could think about it anymore, Annie went over the edge of the half-pipe.

Right away, she was sure she was going to die! The wind whooshed right through her clothes as she went down. A second later she was going up the other side and slowing down big time. No way could she make it to the top. She suddenly realized that once the momentum stopped, she'd go back down — backward! Just as her speed was about to give out, Annie turned 180 degrees and went down face forward. There were no panicked thoughts this time. She only made it halfway up the pipe before she turned again. Then one more time up and down before she stopped at the bottom.

She glanced up at Jesse at the top of the half-pipe. "I must be crazy. I want to do that again!"

"Sure, but it's my turn now." Jesse launched off the half-pipe as soon as Annie got out of the way. He zoomed down faster than Annie had and when he made it to the top on the other side, he brought his knees to his chest and grabbed the underside of the board while completing a 360-degree turn in mid-air. He landed back on the pipe and returned to the other side where he started.

Half the kids at the park cheered, but none louder than Annie. That was incredible.

Annie and Lexie spent the rest of the afternoon hanging out with skater boys, roller girls, and anyone else who showed up with wheels or without. It was an amazing afternoon.

When Annie got home that night, totally exhausted but feeling better than ever, she knew what she had to do.

She couldn't debate it anymore. In fact, there was nothing to debate.

She opened her laptop and wrote an email to Kelsey and the cheerleading coach.

Thanks for selecting me to be a part of the squad. Unfortunately, I'm not going to join at this time as it conflicts with my roller derby training. Good luck with the season ahead.

Sincerely,

Annie

She hit "send" and grinned. Who cared if Kelsey thought she was a freak? Annie was going to be a roller girl!

Chapter 14

Annie walked down the hall on Monday feeling great. She couldn't believe how much the cheerleading acceptance had been weighing her down. She really hadn't wanted to join the squad.

If she had known how easy it would be to send that email, and how good she'd feel afterward, she would have done it sooner.

Sure, Dad had been disappointed, but that was only because he was worried about her. She had explained to him that with Kelsey on the squad, cheerleading was more dangerous than he thought.

So Annie was in a fantastic mood as she headed to class. Kelsey wasn't on her mind at all anymore.

Until Annie ran into her.

Actually, Kelsey ran into Annie. Just as Kelsey walked by, she performed the fakest trip possible and practically threw her iced coffee with whipped cream all over Annie.

"Oh dear, I'm *so* sorry," Kelsey said in the phoniest English accent Annie had ever heard. Her subordinates pointed and laughed.

Annie wiped the cream from her eyes. Only a bit landed on her face; thankfully it didn't sting. The rest of the drink had gone down her front. There were at least two ice cubes nestled in her bra. She shifted her shirt and bra to extract the invasive ice pieces before they did any damage.

"What was that for?" Annie yelled.

"Because you deserve it," Kelsey said.

Annie shook her head to clear it. "Wha —"

"No one, and I mean *no one*, turns down being a cheerleader. Is it because you think you're too good for us? With your stuck-up accent and your punk tastes? Well, you're not." Kelsey shoved Annie's shoulder like they did on television before a fistfight. "Because let me tell you, you're going to regret turning us down."

"Look, it's —" Annie really wished she knew how to respond. And how to make Kelsey listen.

"You're such a snob. And you're not that good at gymnastics. Coach only wanted you for affirmative action or something stupid like that."

A hand brushed Annie's shoulder and the blob of whipped cream that had been there went flying straight at Kelsey's face. "Get lost before I kick your pathetic cheerleading ass!" someone yelled.

Annie blinked a couple of times. That couldn't be Holly.

It was. Short, feisty Holly, looking like she was ready to pounce on Kelsey and tear her to pieces.

"How dare you!" Kelsey screeched as she wiped the cream from her cheek. "I'm going straight to the principal."

"You threw the coffee on me," Annie said. It wasn't the best comeback but at least she'd finally managed to defend herself.

"Do us all a favor and go back to London, and take the leprechaun with you." Kelsey turned away with a mighty swing of her hair, her two subordinates copying her to perfection.

Holly responded by scooping up a handful of ice from the floor and throwing the cubes like darts to the back of their heads. "Oh yeah, come back and say that to my face, you witch."

Several chunks of ice hit their backs, but the cheerleaders didn't turn back around. They sped up.

Holly shook her head. Then she grabbed Annie's arm and dragged her to the bathroom. "Let's get you cleaned up," she said.

In the bathroom, Holly grabbed some paper towels and tried to wipe away some of the coffee. Not that it helped. There was still a huge brown stain on Annie's soaking-wet pink shirt.

"That stain's not going anywhere without a washing machine." Holly handed her a paper towel.

Annie took it slowly. While part of her worried that Holly was just going to play a meaner trick on her than Kelsey had, the other part wondered if she had misjudged Holly.

But no one could be meaner than Kelsey. It was worth trusting Holly.

"Thanks," she said. "You didn't have to stand up for me."

Holly pulled out her makeup bag, avoiding Annie's gaze. "Trust me, I know."

"I thought you didn't like me." Annie wet more paper towels.

Holly focused on her reflection as she retouched her eyeliner. "Who says I do?" Then she shrugged. "The fact is, you're one of us now and no one messes with my roller girls."

Annie smiled. It wasn't exactly a vow of friendship, but she could live with that. "Thanks."

"Yeah, well, just don't make me regret it." Holly rolled her newly made-up eyes, but there was a slight smile on her face. Annie relaxed a little more.

The bathroom door opened and in walked Liz. She took in Annie's stained shirt and Holly's nonchalance and looked worried. "What happened?"

"Kelsey," Annie said. She sighed, still dabbing at

her shirt. "She was a bit annoyed that I chose roller derby over cheerleading."

"Annoyed?" Holly snorted. "She went psycho."

"That's a better way to put it," Annie admitted. "She said no one turned down cheerleading."

"I did." Liz shrugged. "Three years ago, before Kelsey was at the school. It was a different crowd back then, with some really nice girls but I decided it wasn't my thing. I wanted to be part of the game, not just cheer from the sidelines."

That's easy for you, Annie thought.

Liz wasn't the type who would take being bullied. She was cool just for being who she was.

Annie threw away the paper towels. They hadn't done much good. She'd have to wear a wet and stained shirt for the rest of the day, unless she felt like raiding the lost and found again.

"I just wish I knew why Kelsey hates me so much," she said. "I ran into her on my first day here and supposedly ruined her outfit, and she's been horrible to me ever since. And I didn't even mean to. It was an accident. Really."

"If I had bumped into her, it wouldn't have been an accident." Holly puckered at her reflection to apply more lipstick.

Liz placed a comforting hand on Annie's shoulder. "She's obviously intimidated by you. The only way she can deal with it is to be nasty."

"Why? I can't even come up with a good comeback."

Holly set down her makeup and raised an eyebrow at Annie. "Yeah, we need to work on that."

"You're new and foreign," Liz said, "and therefore more interesting. You're also prettier and skinnier than her, which in her mind, counts for everything. And you're by far a better gymnast."

Annie narrowed her eyes. "How do you know?"

Liz grinned. "I saw the tryouts. My little sister wanted to be a cheerleader. She didn't make it. I've tried to get her into derby, but it's not her scene. It'd be awesome if we could put some of your gymnastics moves into derby, but that'd be too dangerous."

Holly finished primping and sighed. "Trust me, I'd give anything to double axel over the pack. Just can't get enough height."

Annie and Liz grinned at each other. Any height Holly lacked, she made up for in attitude.

"Thanks, both of you," Annie said. "It's so nice to be part of a team again." She looked down at her shirt. It was still wet and stained. If rumors spread as easily as they did at her old school, everyone was going to know what had happened.

Annie bit her lip. She wasn't going to cry. Not in front of Liz and Holly. They'd take back everything and think she wasn't tough enough to be a teammate. She stared at the floor, hoping they didn't notice she was about to break down.

Liz gave her shoulders a squeeze. "Hey, look, I have an extra shirt in my bag. Might be a little smelly, but at least it's dry."

Annie took a deep breath and gratefully accepted the shirt. She took off hers and put on Liz's. It was a baggy black one, but it didn't smell at all, despite what Liz said. Annie took another breath. She felt much better now.

She glanced at the mirror. She wasn't going to win any beauty contests today, but the borrowed shirt at least gave her more confidence. And no matter what, it was better than having Tyler see her covered in coffee and whipped cream.

Liz held open the door and the three headed out toward class. "Look, forget about Kelsey," she said. "You're one of us now. We're a good crowd, you'll see. And we got your back. Trust me, no one messes with a derby girl."

Chapter 15

Annie got to the roller rink, laced up her skates, and sprinted five laps around the rink before she felt human again. The morning's Kelsey coffee catastrophe had been on her mind all day. She couldn't stop thinking about what Kelsey had said. *"You're such a snob."* Annie was glad to finally have a distraction.

There were way more people at the rink than Annie expected. At least forty. There were some girls she recognized from school or the Fresh Meat workshop, but most of them were new to her.

"Are there really this many girls on the team?" Annie asked Lauren, who was skating next to her.

"This is the whole league. There are four teams in the league. We play with them and against them."

"That's a bit odd, isn't it?" Annie asked, though she remembered in the Illinoisies' bout how everyone seemed to be friends rather than rivals.

"That's roller derby for you," Lauren explained. "Teams in a league usually practice together, unless they're too far away."

A brown-haired girl with wide hips and a tiny waist skated past them, switched direction, and skated backward while talking to them. "Hi, I'm Carmen, a Liberty Belle. Do you know what team you're on?"

Annie and Lauren shook their heads.

"Go find out." Carmen jerked her head to the wall. "Coach Ritter put up the rosters."

Annie and Lauren looked at each other and raced toward the wall. Annie got there a second before Lauren and did a perfect tomahawk stop in front of the list. She found her name on the third list, along with Lauren's and about eleven others. They were Liberty Belles too, still coached by Coach Ritter, and Liz was their captain. Brilliant. Holly was also a Belle. That was good. Even though Annie and Holly were cool now, she wouldn't have liked competing against her; the bruise on her thigh from their crash last week was still the size of Wales.

Lauren linked her arm through Annie's and stood tall. Even so, she only reached just above Annie's shoulder. "Now you can officially be my wife."

Annie shook her head and smiled. "What?"

Lauren let go but kept a mischievous gleam in her eye. "Derby wives. Good friends that have each other's backs and are there for the other in a jam. Whatcha think?"

Why not? Annie thought. Lauren was a great roller girl and Annie really liked hanging out with her. Besides, it was all in good fun. "I think I better tell my parents I've gotten hitched."

Lauren laughed and punched her on the shoulder.

The Prairie Girls' coach, Shanti Morningstar, called everyone to the middle. Her thick blond dreadlocks bouncing, she said, "Welcome! Today we're playing a variation on tag called Jaws. We're starting with one shark and the rest of you are fish. If the shark catches you, you become a shark too and need to skate over here and put on a helmet panty so the fish can avoid you. If you skate out of bounds, as a fish or shark, you're out of the game. Newbies, really keep an eye out. It's your responsibility not to get tagged *and* to avoid crashing into anyone. Sharmila, you wanted to be the first shark."

A gorgeous girl with brown skin, green eyes, and black hair glided to the middle of the rink and beamed. With her perfect glittering makeup, designer skirt, and workout shirt, Annie would have thought she was a Bollywood star, not a roller girl. She hadn't been part of the Fresh Meat group, so that must mean she'd been in the league for a while. Annie had the feeling that in this girl's case, looks were deceiving.

She was right. As soon as the whistle blew,

Sharmila proved that being gorgeous didn't mean she wasn't tough. Within ten seconds, she had tagged three people. Now with four sharks on the loose, and about forty people trying to get away, Annie really had to concentrate. There were so many girls, skating in every different direction. Twice she almost got forced out of bounds, but just managed to turn sharply to avoid getting tagged. Every once in a while a whistle would blow and a coach would signal a girl out of the game for going out of bounds.

Annie spotted Carmen coming up behind her, so she twisted away across the rink. Her head whipped around in every direction, keeping an eye out for skaters wearing helmet covers. Carmen whizzed past, switched targets, and pelted across to a girl with short black pigtails.

The fish were dwindling and the sharks were gaining force. Half of the girls, including Lauren and Liz, had been sent off for going out of bounds. There were only about five fish left in the entire sea. And Holly the Shark locked her eyes on a British delicacy.

Annie stared at Holly for a second before a small grin crept over her face. She knew Holly was competitive, but Holly probably didn't know that she was, too. At the same instant Holly lunged at her, Annie sprinted off. She darted from one end to the other, weaving around other sharks who were after the remaining fish, but there was no shaking off Holly.

Annie felt a hand brush across her arm. She'd been caught. Holly wore a smug smile, but she nodded to show that she was impressed with Annie's performance.

The rest of the fish were caught before Annie had a chance to put on her helmet cover.

"Great work, everyone," Coach Ritter said. She and the other coaches clapped. "Now let's work with packs of blockers, passing them and going through. Four separate packs on each side of the rink. Carmen, Bea, Lauren, and Annie, form a wall over here. Holly, you're jammer."

The four got together and Carmen took charge. "Have you two been part of the pack yet?"

Annie and Lauren shook their heads. Annie gulped. She was not looking forward to this.

Carmen slipped on a helmet cover with a broad stripe. "I'll pivot, which means I set the pace and call orders. You three stay with me. If we spread apart, she can pass us easily. If we're a solid wall, we can hold her back."

Coach Morningstar blew her whistle. Lauren squatted down to her derby stance and looked so intimidating there was no way any jammer would try getting past her. Annie tried to copy Lauren, but she knew the result was more like a rabbit glaring at headlights than intimidation.

The whistle blew again and Holly charged toward them. In just a matter of seconds, Annie had to focus on skating with the pack and keeping Holly from scoring. She couldn't imagine what it'd be like with five more players on the track. How could she possibly play offense and defense at the same time?

Annie, holding onto Lauren's hips, did what Carmen had suggested to block Holly. It didn't work. Holly passed them as if they weren't even blocking her way. And just to prove her point, she cut through the middle of the rink, got behind, and passed them again without even trying.

"Newbie," Carmen called to Annie. "Don't be afraid to block her. Your job is to not let her get by."

Annie nodded. She understood what she needed to do, though she wasn't really sure she could put it into action.

"It's okay, wifey." Lauren punched her on the shoulder. "Just got to work on being more solid."

Easy for her to say. Lauren was about as solid as they got. Annie hadn't seen her get knocked over once.

She tried blocking a few more times with different people as jammers. She was getting better; she actually blocked a couple of girls and when they broke through, it wasn't because of her. But they were newbies too.

When it was her turn as jammer, Annie was determined to prove her worth. Crouched low, she pushed off and ran on her toe stops as soon as her whistle blew. She reached the pack in an instant but couldn't get through. Derby wife or not, Lauren wasn't going to make it easy for her. And Holly might only weigh a hundred pounds, but she was super quick and in the way whenever Annie tried to pass. She only just managed to get past another newbie when the whistle blew, signaling that the two minutes were up.

"Good job, everyone. Take five, grab a breather," Coach Ritter called out and motioned for Annie to come toward her.

Annie took a deep breath. She was being kicked

off. Coach realized she had made a mistake and Annie didn't really have the skills to play.

"Go get your skates checked out, Annie. I think your wheel bearings might need cleaning." Coach Ritter pointed to Jesse behind the skate rental booth.

Annie let out a sigh of relief. She wasn't being booted off.

Yet.

She took off her skates and handed them to Jesse to clean up. He whistled when he gave a wheel a test spin. "Yup, they need some juice for sure. So, have you come up with a cool derby name?"

Annie shook her head. "No, I haven't thought about it really. Have you got any ideas?"

His face lit up as he cleaned the skates. "Tons. I-Tarzan U-Pain, Lady Gagya, Buffy the Tramp Slayer, Sin Bin McQuinn. If you were Lexie, you could be Lex Lethal."

Annie knew her best friend well enough that if she were a roller girl, her name would be something along the lines of Freaka Kahlo.

"What would your name be, if you played?" Annie asked.

Jesse didn't even pause to think about it. "Death Vader. It's my ref name."

"I guess I want something I can relate to. That says who I am." Annie pulled out her hairband to redo her ponytail.

"What about Hairy Slaughter?"

Annie pushed him lightly on the arm. "I don't have that much hair."

In response, Jesse tried to blow his own hair out of his blue eyes before handing back her skates. Annie took hold of her skates slowly. He really had gorgeous eyes. With his hair covering his face most of the time, his eyes were easy to overlook.

"All right, let's get back to work," Coach Ritter called.

Annie laced up quickly and rejoined everyone on the rink. The difference in her skates was unbelievable. It felt like she could turn just by thinking about it. Now if that would only help her blocking, she'd be in good shape.

Over the sound system came the Sex Pistols' song, "Anarchy in the UK."

Great song, Jesse, Annie thought. She was singing the lyrics in her head when it hit her.

Anarchy.

Anne R. Key.

She couldn't help it. Even though the coaches

had called them over to the middle, she had to tell him first. Jesse saw her racing to him and leaned over the barrier. "Skates too slick?" he asked.

Annie shook her head with a huge smile and pointed to the speakers. "That's me. That's my derby name. Anne R. Key!"

"Sweet! That's definitely you." He gave her a high five and cranked the volume higher.

Annie spun around and soared back to the group. Of course Jesse would think it was brilliant. He'd named his mutt Sid Vicious.

"Let's hold a scrimmage. Liberty Belles versus Prairie Girls and High Rollers versus Derby Dolls. Each set of teams will skate one jam on, one jam off. Jesse, if you're free, we could use you as a jam ref." One of the coaches waved his clipboard. Jesse nodded. In less than a minute he'd hopped over the barrier in battered quad skates, a whistle swinging around his neck.

Annie watched the first couple of jams from the bench. At the Illinoisies' bout she hadn't fully appreciated how chaotic it all was. It was impossible to watch what everyone was doing. Girls went every which way and the coach refs kept sending players to the penalty box for things Annie couldn't figure out. When Coach Ritter put her out as a blocker, it dawned on Annie that she was finally going to play roller derby, even if it was just a scrimmage.

She huddled next to Lauren. That had to work. No one could get by Lauren.

Right?

The whistle blew and the jammers sprinted toward the pack. Annie looked over her left shoulder, over her right, over her left again. The Prairie Girl jammer, LaTicia, was right at her side, trying to barge her way through. But Lauren was also at Annie's side, and she wasn't budging. LaTicia darted to Annie's other side. One of the opposing blockers got in Annie's way, allowing LaTicia to slip right through. Jesse blew his whistle twice to indicate LaTicia was the lead jammer and followed her from the middle of the rink with his arms in an L-shape. Holly got through the pack seconds later.

"Newbie," Carmen shouted to Annie. "You can block other players too. Not just the jammer."

"And don't forget to move. You're on skates, use them," Liz added.

Annie crouched low and looked over her shoulder. LaTicia was seconds away. Carmen and Lauren huddled around Annie. She felt the jammer push against her and she pushed back. LaTicia tried the other side and Annie didn't let her through that way either. She knew it was because her teammates were glued to her side, but Annie was glad she managed a good block.

The Prairie Girls' pivot came to rescue LaTicia. Annie got ready for a big booty-block swing at the pivot.

And landed on her hands and knees.

That wasn't nearly as bad as I thought it'd be.

She pushed herself up and returned quickly to the pack. Just because LaTicia had passed her didn't mean she had to give up. Moments later, Annie booty-blocked LaTicia out of bounds before she could score more points. LaTicia quickly called off the jam.

When Jesse blew the whistle, Annie welcomed the quick break while the High Rollers and Derby Dolls took the track. Her hair was plastered with sweat underneath the helmet. That was much more tiring than she had expected.

And so much fun!

In their next jam, Lauren was the jammer. "Who's got my panty?" she shouted with a grin before someone threw her the starred helmet cover.

As Annie watched Lauren slip the panty over her helmet, she felt a twinge of jealousy. Lauren was great — Annie had agreed to be her derby wife after all — but they had started at the same time. When would it be Annie's turn to be the jammer?

Coach Ritter seemed to know what she was thinking. "You have to learn to block before you can be a jammer. Keep working on it."

Annie did. She was put in as a blocker for a few more jams. Jammers still sneaked right by her but at least she could delay them now. In one brilliant jam, Annie, Sharmila, and two other girls managed to hold off the jammer while Holly almost danced on her toe stops to get in front and become the lead.

Soon, Annie thought. *Soon, I'll be a jammer too.*

She focused on that and it helped with her blocking. It didn't scare her so much anymore. It helped that she also had a motive.

"Annie, good improvement," Coach Ritter said as they skated off to let the other two teams play. "If you're not too tired, why don't you try being jammer for the next jam."

Holly threw her the helmet panty. "Look, the secret isn't to barge your way through. It's to find opportunities, even the smallest, and grab them."

Annie gave her a smile. "Thanks."

Holly rolled her eyes as if to say whatever, but then smiled back.

Annie got ready behind the pack and was out running as soon as she heard the sound of the second whistle. She headed straight for the center of the pack. If she could just duck between them . . .

Wait, was there a gap to the side?

Yes!

She squeezed through and she was past the pack. Jesse had his arms in an L-shape and was grinning so much the whistle slipped out of his mouth. That meant she was the lead jammer!

With a great burst, Annie raced around the track. The other jammer, she knew, was not far behind. If she could only make it through the pack again, she could call off the jam before the other jammer scored points.

When Annie had nearly reached the pack, Carmen held out her arm. Annie knew what to do — she'd seen the Illinoisies do it.

With a mighty swing, Carmen whipped her to the front of the pack. Or what had been the front. In a flash, the Prairie Girls' pivot was in front, breaking Annie's momentum. With no time to change direction, Annie crashed smack into the pivot. The two hit the floor hard, along with Carmen and two others whose limbs could be seen flailing about. It was a pile-up.

And it was all Annie's fault.

Annie scrambled back to her feet and called off the jam before the other jammer could score more points, but it had been a total disaster. She knew she wouldn't be picked as jammer anytime soon.

How could she have thought she was good at something again?

Chapter 16

Unsurprisingly, Coach Ritter didn't play Annie as jammer again at the next practice, but she made sure Annie got a lot of time blocking.

"You have to learn to block before you can be a jammer." Coach Ritter's words played like a mantra in Annie's head. If that's what it took, she was going to do it. Breaking through the pack and skating around the rink at top speed was a thrill she hadn't felt since she retired from the uneven bars.

She got Lauren to stay with her after practice on Thursday to work on the blocking. Finally, after half an hour of extra practice, they made it around the rink with Annie blocking Lauren and not letting her pass. "I really think you're getting the hang of it," Lauren said, unclipping her helmet.

"Thanks for the help. I couldn't have done it without you." Annie took off her own helmet and crumpled onto the bench.

"No sweat." Lauren wiped her drenched forehead and laughed. "That's what derby wives are for."

"Do you think I'll get a chance to play jammer on Saturday?" Annie asked.

Saturday was their first bout. Just thinking about it terrified her.

Lauren shrugged. "Coach seems really fair. If she thinks you can to do it, she'll let you."

Annie sighed. She'd been skating everywhere around town to build up her endurance and she felt better at practice, but Coach hadn't seemed to notice. On the other hand, she hadn't criticized Annie's blocking, so maybe that was a good sign.

"Hey, I just remembered," Lauren said. "What's your playing number going to be?" She peeled off the zebra-patterned duct tape securing her kneepads.

Annie frowned. She hadn't thought of a number. "Won't Coach just give me a random number no one else has?"

"Not in derby. You can be creative and can use let-ters, symbols, whatever. Liz's number is '1000rpm,' Holly is '97lbs.' There's a woman in the adult league who's '-0' and another who's '50ish.' She's actually fifty-six years old and still playing derby!"

If Annie were a roller girl in her fifties, she'd brag about it too. "What's yours?"

Lauren grinned, clearly feeling proud of herself. "10^{24}."

"That's a massive number," Annie said. "Why did you pick it?"

"It's a yottabyte. Makes megabytes and gigabytes on computers look like babies, an inside computer-nerd joke. I love it. That's the thing with derby numbers. They should mean something to you."

If that was the case, Annie needed to give her number more thought. She'd always liked the number 96 — it was the same upside down and it was the year her parents got married — but that seemed boring after "50ish."

Lauren had finished packing up all her things. Annie noticed a hoodie on top of the lockers and brought it down. "Is this yours too?"

"Yeah, thanks. I forgot I threw it up there." Lauren pulled on the black hoodie covered in brown and white dog hair.

Annie shrugged. "That's what derby wives are for. At least tall ones."

"I like tall girls. What can I say, I've got good taste." Lauren smiled. "See ya."

Annie waved and gathered up the last of her things. People didn't often compliment her on her height. It was nice. She had gotten so used to everyone saying how unfortunate her height was for gymnastics that she never really thought about it as an asset. She stood up straight and pulled her shoulders back. Why shouldn't she feel proud of being five foot eleven and a half? It was just a number.

Number!

With a new burst of energy, Annie skated home at top speed. She knew exactly what her derby number would be.

Saturday arrived suddenly. But before Annie's first bout that evening was an event just as exciting: Rosie Lee's grand opening.

Annie got to the café at eight in the morning. Everything looked perfect. The tables and chairs looked inviting, the whole place was spotless, and Lexie's mural was eye-catching enough to attract attention from people passing by outside.

And that was all nothing compared to the gorgeous displays of scones, croissants, cupcakes, muffins, tarts, cakes, and cookies (they weren't British, but there were no good cookies in town — both Annie and Dad had checked).

Dad had been baking since four in the morning. He was just finishing the sandwiches when Annie got there.

"The place looks great, Dad. I'm really proud of you."

Dad leaned over and kissed her on top of her head. "Same here, Beanie."

Annie checked the coffee, regular and decaf. Done. Hot water tap. On.

"Are you ready?" Annie asked, slapping her thighs like a drum roll. Dad tied on a clean apron and took a deep breath before nodding.

With a flamboyant gesture, Annie flipped the sign from Closed to Open.

She let out her breath and smoothed out invisible creases on the tablecloths. "So what can I do?"

"Glad you asked," Dad said. "I printed some coupons I want you to hand out. Free coffee or tea with every pastry or sandwich. What do you think?"

Annie held an invisible microphone to her mouth and put on a deep movie-voiceover accent. "David Turner was just a small town boy until the day his baking changed life in Liberty Heights forever."

Dad bowed and blew kisses at the imaginary

crowd. "I'd like to thank everyone who made this moment possible, especially my gods Dionysus and Edesia. And I suppose my daughter, too, if I must."

Annie threw a packet of sugar at him.

Dad laughed and pulled her into a tight hug. "You're the best, Beanie."

"You're okay too, I guess," Annie teased before pulling away. "I'm going to grab my Rollerblades. That way I can zoom all over town passing out the coupons."

Dad ducked back into the kitchen and wiped down the clean counter. "Well, I was hoping you'd do me another favor," he said.

"Why aren't you looking at me? Is it something awful?" Annie crossed her arms.

Dad adjusted the wrapping on a sandwich. "Not awful. I thought it'd be fun. See, since it's a British-style café, I got you something to wear while you hand out the coupons."

"Okay," Annie said nervously. "But it better not be a Union Jack dress."

Dad didn't answer. Instead he pulled out something covered in dry-cleaning plastic. "They didn't have many options at the costume store. It was either this or James Bond."

"It can't be too bad if 007 was the other option," Annie said.

Wrong. The dress was frumpy with a matching handbag and came with a short, curly gray wig and a crown.

"The Queen? You want me to dress like the Queen?" she said. "Bond would have been a much better choice."

Dad started rushing around, searching for something to do. "I looked for a Kate Middleton-type dress but there wasn't anything that would let people know who you were without explaining it."

Annie didn't think many people here would know she was the Queen, either. "Do I have to wear this?"

"It's not that bad, is it?"

Annie bit her lip. "It's just — well, it's a little embarrassing."

Dad forced a smile. "No, if you don't want to that's okay. I just thought it'd be fun and help bring attention to the café."

When he put it that way, Annie couldn't say no. "All right, then. But I'm still wearing my Rollerblades."

The bells attached to the front door jingled and

an old woman with blue hair poked her head in. "The sign says you're open."

"That we are!" Dad darted over and opened the door the rest of the way for his first customer.

By the time Annie left, dressed like Queen Elizabeth II on Rollerblades, there were three more people in the café and Dad already knew them all by name.

Everyone outside who passed by turned to glance at Annie; it wasn't every day a booty-blocking queen whirled around Liberty Heights. She hated all the stares, but kept reminding herself it was for Dad as she smiled and handed out coupons.

"Are you a real queen?" asked a little girl.

Annie didn't know how to answer that. She didn't want to lie, but she didn't want to be the one to tell the little girl that people in costumes weren't always real.

Instead, she changed the subject. "What's your name?"

"Clara," the little girl said.

Annie crouched on her skates to get to her level. "Clara! That's pretty. Would you like to try on my crown?"

The little girl nodded enthusiastically. Annie

placed the crown on her hair and smiled as the girl's mother took a picture.

"What do you say, Clara?" her mother urged when Annie placed the crown back on her wig.

"Thank you, your majesty," Clara said, curtsying.

Annie smiled and skated off. Okay, maybe the outfit wasn't that bad.

She soon figured out who were the best people to approach with coupons, and who to avoid. Businessy types crossed to the other side of the street when they saw her coming. People on phones just threw the coupon away without looking at it. Mothers with four young kids heading to the barbershop also didn't need a distraction.

But retired men on benches, people strolling leisurely, and anybody else who had the time for a ten-second chat about Rosie Lee's got a coupon.

When she got back to the café to replenish her coupons, Annie was glad to see that it was busy. Dad was running from one place to the other with a huge grin on his face, barely keeping up with everything that needed doing. Annie jumped in to brew a new pot of coffee, empty the dishwasher, and put six cupcakes in a white bakery box for Clara and her mother.

"I hope you know you'll have to wear that costume again," Clara's mother said. "Clara will be devastated otherwise." She winked and Clara waved until they turned the corner.

Annie waved back, but inside she was wincing. She didn't want to disappoint a sweet little girl, but she hoped she never had to see the costume again.

She grabbed some more coupons, but as she was leaving, she spotted Lexie and her parents sitting at a table with a proper cream tea. That meant English breakfast tea served with scones, strawberry jam, sliced strawberries, and fresh clotted cream, which Dad had made himself. Next to them was a box that held a sample of some other treats. On the house, of course.

"Hey, Annie, great look." Lexie grinned, but knowing Lexie's taste in fashion (today, even though it was getting chilly, she was in a Hawaiian-print dress with a flower in her hair), Annie couldn't tell if she was being sarcastic or serious. Lexie pointed at Annie's Rollerblades and added, "I'm not sure about the footwear, though."

Sarcasm. "Next time *you* wear the dress," Annie said with a laugh, and I'll keep the skates."

Lexie's eyes lit up. "Bring it."

Dad came over to the table during a quick pause of the madness. "Thanks for coming, guys. Always a pleasure to have you here. Everyone has been asking me about the mural, Lexie." He turned to Mr. and Mrs. Jones and added, "You have a very talented daughter."

"Thanks," Mrs. Jones said.

Mr. Jones added, "And Annie is such a joy."

Annie blushed, but Dad smiled. "I know."

The doorbells jingled and Dad ran off to tend to the next customers.

"I better go too. Dad printed five hundred coupons that I have to hand out," Annie said. "See you later tonight?" she asked Lexie.

"Wouldn't miss it." Lexie hugged Annie. Then she pulled a large bag out from under the table. "Here, this is for you. Don't open it until you get to the rink."

"Ooh, a present? Thanks, Lex."

Annie stashed the bag in the kitchen before skating off with more coupons.

But just like some horrible kind of déjà vu, Annie turned the corner and encountered her worst nightmare. She didn't jump over a dog and crash into someone's yogurt, but it was just as bad. There, right in front of her, surrounded by friends, was Kelsey. With Tyler at her side.

Annie quickly changed direction, but she wasn't quick enough.

"Annie," Tyler called.

Face glowing, wig and crown suddenly feeling very heavy, Annie slowly turned back around. With a deep breath, she skated toward them and gave Tyler a coupon.

"'British-style café,'" Tyler read from the paper in his hand. "I thought British food was kind of gross."

He was teasing, she knew that, but it still stung a bit. "We've come a long way since the olden days," she said, trying to sound relaxed.

"Not far enough," said Kelsey, jutting out a hip. "Or they would have taught you something about fashion."

"Hey, lay off, Kels," Tyler said. "Annie's just wearing that to help promote her dad's café." A panicked look suddenly crossed his face. "I mean, that's not how you always dress on the weekend, right, Annie?"

"Right," she agreed, though she would have agreed with Tyler about anything at that moment.

He had stood up for her! Against Kelsey! "See you at school." She held up her coupons in a wave and started to skate away.

"Wait," Kelsey said. "Don't I get one?"

Annie did a T-stop and glanced from her coupons to Kelsey. "I wouldn't have thought you needed any cakes, Kelsey, seeing as you're so sweet already." Her voice was dripping with sarcasm. Everyone, except Kelsey, laughed as she skated away.

Annie gave herself an internal high-five. She shouldn't have stooped to Kelsey's level, but it certainly felt good finally getting one up on her.

Annie helped out in the busy café for most of the afternoon. Toward the end of the day, when things got quieter, she skated around downtown again to hand out more coupons.

Just before five o'clock, Annie returned to Rosie Lee's, coupons all gone. There was one customer left, enjoying late afternoon treacle tart and tea, and an energetic chat with Dad about being an American in London. Annie wriggled out of her queen garb in the bathroom, grateful that the costume shop hadn't included a corset, and then headed into the kitchen and helped herself to one of the leftover sandwiches. By the time she'd finished, the last customer was gone, as were the remaining slices of the tart.

"Good day, yeah?" Annie asked as she poured out the coffee and cleaned the containers.

Dad's eyes shone as he changed the sign from Open to Closed.

"The best, Beanie," he said. "We ran out of the lemon and mascarpone scones by noon. The anise shortbread disappeared after I gave away some samples. And that last guy, Simon, took the rest of the treacle tart home to his family and wants me to make the cake for his six-year-old's birthday party."

"That's great, Dad. I'm really glad."

A car outside honked. Annie looked at the clock and knew it was time. "That's Liz. She's taking me to the bout. You're coming, right?"

They looked around the empty café. There was so much cleaning to do — and the display case was almost empty.

Dad sighed. "I don't know, Beanie. There's a lot I have to do before tomorrow. But I'll try."

Annie gave him a hug before grabbing Lexie's surprise bag and running out to the car. Her stomach was in knots and she knew it was more than just nerves.

She really hoped Dad would make it. He had been to every single one of her gymnastics meets. It was Mum, never Dad, who always had to work late.

One workaholic parent was bad enough. She didn't want to think what it'd be like to have two.

Chapter 17

In the locker room, a black and red T-shirt came flying toward Annie's head. She caught it with one hand. Straightening it out, she couldn't stop staring at it. The front had Lady Liberty in derby gear with a tough scowl on her face, but the back was the best:

Anne R. Key. 5'11 ½"

Perfect.

She put it on along with a pair of fishnets she and Lexie had bought and her lucky silver gymnastics shorts. Using a black eyeliner, Lauren wrote "5'11½" on Annie's arms and Annie wrote Lauren's number on hers. Pads and skates on. Mouth guard and helmet at hand. She was ready to go.

"Annie, where are you going?" Sharmila said.

"Just heading out to look at the crowd."

But Sharmila shook her head and pointed back at the bench. "Not without your face." Sharmila sat in front of her and began applying makeup. "I'm going for fierce sparkle with you."

Annie didn't know how to argue, and she wasn't sure she wanted to. Girls in gymnastics always plastered on the makeup. It was kind of like preparing for battle.

She looked around at the other girls. Holly looked like a Hollywood starlet with 1930s makeup and freshly dyed flame-red hair. Liz had a green painted mask that resembled a butterfly. Lauren was done up with two black streaks under her eyes like a football player — she had refused anything that looked remotely girly, though her mid-thigh shorts were hot pink.

When Sharmila handed Annie a mirror, she couldn't believe what she saw. She wouldn't have thought to give herself that look, but the result was amazing: nastily cool scars on one side and stars on the other with almost as much glitter as Sharmila herself.

"All right, peeps." Coach Ritter came in with a clipboard and her long auburn hair pulled into two low pigtails. "I know we were bottom of the league last year, but we've got a killer team now, so let's show them what we got. Warm-ups in two minutes."

As Annie stood up, she remembered Lexie's surprise package.

She gasped when she opened the bag. Lexie had gotten her a helmet and decorated it with a Warhol-esque portrait of Annie. It was utterly amazing.

Lauren leaned over. "Wow. Did you paint that yourself?"

Annie shook her head as she strapped it on. "My best friend, Lexie, is a brilliant artist."

"I'll say," Lauren said. "That's amazing."

The team skated onto the rink to warm up. There weren't very many people there and Annie quickly found Lexie waving a banner painted with old-fashioned house keys and the words, "Total Anne R. Key!"

Annie waved, pointed to her helmet, and shouted, "It's perfect. Cheers."

Lexie responded by waving her banner more.

Annie kept skating around. She saw Jesse by the sound system and a few kids she recognized from school. But no Dad.

He'll come. He's never let me down.

But Annie couldn't help but worry that this would be the first time.

Liz had them do some stretches before gathering them around by the sidelines. "Everyone looks great. Remember that blocking we've been working on, but most of all don't forget to have fun."

They cheered and sat on the benches.

"Good evening, roller derby fans," Jesse said into the loudspeaker. "Tonight's bout is between the Liberty Belles and the Derby Dolls!"

Both teams cheered. Maybe it was Annie's imagination, but there seemed to be a considerably louder cheer from their team and supporters. If Dad were here, he'd put cheerleaders to shame with his booming voice.

Then it was time to introduce the skaters.

"She might only be ninety-seven pounds, but watch out for Holly Terr-rror!" Jesse said. Holly skated around the rink backward and did a jump like figure skaters on television, landing on one skate.

"Feel the love as Sharmila the Hun sends out those XOXOs!" Sharmila didn't skate around, but stood blowing kisses at the crowd and looking gorgeous as always.

"And here comes your Liberty Belle captain, going at one thousands revs per minute, make way for ElizaDEATH!" Liz skated around the track, then dropped to one knee and spun around.

As Lauren skated onto the track, her face beaming, Jesse announced, "Time to call the cops, because Lauren Disorder — number ten to the power of twenty-four — is in the house!"

Next it was Annie's turn. "One of the Liberty Belles' newest additions, from London, England, we have number five eleven and a half, Anne R. Key!"

As Jesse introduced the rest of the girls, Annie skated around the track at top speed, stopped, and slid into the splits. As she swung her leg around, she saw a look of surprise — and pain — on several people's faces.

The bout started with Liz as pivot to set the pace and call the plays, three more blockers, Cookie, Bea, and Tashi, and Holly as the jammer. The first whistle blew and the blockers bundled up, moving in the directions dictated by their pivots. When the second whistle went off, Holly dodged a side block from the other jammer as she sprinted toward the pack. As they rounded the first corner, away from the benches, Annie had a hard time watching everything at once. There was so much going on it looked like just a horde of girls on the track. One of the refs sent Hell's Angelica from the other team to the penalty box for elbowing, and Holly sneaked through the gap.

"Holly Terror, first out of the pack, and she's your lead jaaa-mmer!" Jesse announced while the crowd cheered. Holly switched to backward skating and blew kisses toward the crowd as she performed beautiful backward crossovers. She switched to for-ward skating as the other jammer started to catch up. Hell's Angelica came back from the box and the other team had a full number of players in their jam again. With some quick dodging, Holly squeezed through a tiny slot to pass the pack again. From the sideline, Coach Ritter frantically tapped her arms against her hips. Holly responded to the coach's signal and flapped her own arms to call off the jam.

Annie looked at the score. 4-1 in the Liberty Belles' favor.

Sharmila was the next jammer, with Liz still as pivot. They were joined by Lauren, Carmen, and a girl who was in Annie's French class. Carmen and a Derby Doll got sent to the box briefly during that jam. They served their time in the box just as the jam was called off so they didn't have to carry their time over to the next jam. The Derby Dolls' jammer, Polly Socket, scored three points, while Sharmila scored two.

"Natalia, jammer. Holly, pivot. Lauren, Tashi, Annie, get in there," Coach Ritter called out.

Annie took in a sharp breath and skated out onto the rink. This was it.

"Princess," Holly said to Annie. "Watch those gaps."

Annie nodded. She could do this. Just like

practice. She crouched down feeling out of place next to Holly, who was half her size, and Lauren, who was bigger than her.

The second whistle blew, and she looked over her shoulder. The other team's jammer, Mo Jo, was heading her way. Annie remembered her from league practices: Mo liked to sneak by on the outside. Except Lauren had the outside covered and there was no getting by her as she knocked Mo to her knees.

Annie kept her eye on Mo as she quickly got back on her feet. Lauren shifted to the inside to help Natalia get through. Mo came up behind, saw Lauren, and veered quickly to Annie's right. Annie knew what she was going to do and was ready for her. With a mighty swing, Annie booty-blocked Mo and sent her flying out of bounds.

That was fun! Annie thought.

All this time, she had been focusing on being jammer. She hadn't realized how great blocking was.

Lauren showed off her leopard-print mouth guard as she grinned. Together, they blocked the Derby Dolls' blockers, letting Natalia pass and score some points.

Annie stayed on the rink for the next jam, this time with Liz back as pivot and Holly as jammer. Tashi had been sent to the box in the jam before, so they were down one player. Annie was pleased that Coach trusted her enough to keep her in.

"As Holly Terror comes around, ElizaDEATH, Cookie Crumbles, and Anne R. Key form an impenetrable wall," Jesse said into the microphone, talking fast to keep up with all the action. "One player short, they're not letting Slam I. Am sneak by. ElizaDEATH blocks the Dolls' pivot Polly Socket, giving Holly Terror that break to become your lead jammer! Slam I. Am is still trying to find her way through. She tries to get by Anne R. Key, but the newbie is not having it and gives the jammer a mighty block. Holly Terror comes back around. If she passes the whole pack including the other team's jammer, that's a grand slam. Can she do it? Yes! Hey, Slam I. Am, guess what? You've just been grand slaaaammed!"

The Liberty Belles got their player back from the box, who was replaced by Bea, and they played the full two minutes of the jam with Holly racking up fourteen points. Panting as she came off the rink, Annie sat down for her break. The team was playing well, but so were the Derby Dolls, and the scores stayed pretty close. With each jam she played, Annie felt more confident about blocking. When the buzzer sounded for half-time, they were only lagging by two points. In derby scores, that was nothing.

Coach Ritter gathered them together in the locker room. "You're doing great. Everyone's blocking has been right on the money and they're getting worried, I know it. Keep up the great defense, but now we have to up the offense. Help your jammer, and let's show them these Liberty Belles aren't going to be at the bottom of the league this year!"

They all cheered before settling down to fix equipment and makeup. Annie went to the bathroom, drank water, made sure her pads were still secure, and skated back out five minutes before the half-time ended.

She motioned to Lexie to come over to the barrier and gave her a huge hug. "Hey, thanks for the helmet," Annie said. "It's fantastic! All of the girls in the locker room was jealous. I know Sharmila and Bea want theirs painted too."

Lexie looked happy. "Ooh, my first commissions! I got the idea when your dad asked if I was a modern-day Warhol."

Dad.

Annie searched around frantically. With everyone milling about, going to the bathroom, and buying concessions, it was hard to spot people. "Have you seen my dad?" she asked. "Is he here?"

Lexie shook her head. "No. Did he say he was coming?"

Annie didn't answer. She waved at Lexie and started backward skating around the track with a few other girls. The buzzer sounded the end of half-time, and Annie skated over to the bench. Coach Ritter sent her out for the second jam but she stopped dead before getting to the blockers' line. Dashing through the door, hair sticking straight up, shirt covered in flour, and wearing his paint-stained sneakers, was Dad.

He saw her in the rink and shouted, over the music and loudspeaker, "Go, Beanie!"

Annie blushed, then grinned widely. He really was the best dad in the world.

The two teams were still neck and neck. Every time the Belles racked up some points, the Dolls came around to grab them back and get some more. Annie's blocking confidence kept getting better and Coach Ritter sent her out as often as the other players on the team.

Ten minutes to the end of the bout, tensions got high. The score was 98-96 and both teams wanted desperately to win. Penalties flew as they all started playing more aggressively. During one jam, both teams only had three people on the track: a jammer and two blockers.

Three minutes left and the Belles were only lagging by a few points. Annie hadn't bitten her nails in years but suddenly felt she might restart the habit. Liz, Holly, Cookie, and Natalia were all blocking, Sharmila was jammer. No jammer had made it through the pack yet.

"ElizaDEATH is standing her ground as Polly Socket tries to barge through," Jesse announced. "Sharmila the Hun sees an opening, goes for it, but no! Slam I. Am sends her out of bounds."

Sharmila re-entered the track behind the pack and charged. Liz pushed against the opposing blockers to try to make a gap for Sharmila to slip through.

Slam I. Am wasn't having it, though. She shoved back but somehow her legs got in the way, sending Liz flying head over skates. In retaliation, Holly hit Slam illegally with an elbow, and the Derby Doll went crashing to the ground.

A gasp rang through the audience and across the players' bench. Not because of Holly — who was calling Slam a witch, among other things — but because Liz wasn't getting up. The refs blew a time-out and Coach Ritter rushed over to her captain.

"She practically landed on her head," Lauren said as Annie gripped her friend's arm tightly. If anything happened to Liz . . .

The crowd clapped supportively as Coach Ritter and one of the refs helped Liz off the track. Carmen cleared a space for Liz on the bench and offered her a water bottle. Liz's eyes were wide and she seemed a bit dazed but kept saying, "I'm okay, I'm okay."

The Derby Dolls were winning. 2:12 was left on the clock. They'd probably only have time for two more jams, maybe three.

Finally convinced that Liz was okay, or would be, Coach Ritter looked at the girls on the bench. Holly was in the box but so was Slam; both teams would start the jam a player short.

Annie fidgeted. She watched Coach Ritter study the girls sitting on the bench. Carmen had her arm around Liz and didn't look like she was willing to let her go. Sharmila and Natalia had skated two jams in a row and looked tired. With Holly in the box, there wasn't anyone else who normally played jammer.

"Annie, you're jammer. Show us that speed."

Annie looked at her coach with wide eyes before standing up and slipping on the helmet panty someone was holding out to her. She couldn't believe it. She was finally getting her chance. Lauren punched her shoulder and followed her out into the rink with Tashi and Bea.

She could hear Holly screaming encouragement from the box. Dad yelled, "That's my Beanie!" Jesse, who was handling the music as well as MCing, switched from Def Leppard to The Clash's "London Calling."

The jammer next to her was Mo Jo, and by the scowl on her face, it was obvious she hadn't forgotten how Annie had pushed her out of bounds. Annie would have to break away as soon as that whistle blew to get to the pack before Mo. Just like when they were playing Red Light, Green Light, Annie pushed off with her toe stops the split second she heard the whistle blow. She was at the pack in a heartbeat, frantically looking for that gap to squeeze through. Hell's Angelica looked the other way to help Mo. Annie sucked in her breath and slipped by sideways with the heels of her skates together and toes straight out. Hell's Angelica swiveled around to stop her, but Annie was too fast. The jammer ref blew two rapid whistles and pointed at Annie with his arms in an L-shape.

She was the lead jammer! She could hear the crowd screaming and knew that at least two of those voices belonged to Lexie and Dad. Coming up behind the pack, Mo had just broken through and Annie used the same gap to sneak by herself. Mo looked over her shoulder and at that moment, Annie passed her on the outside.

"Unbelievable, folks. Mo Jo has just been grand slammed by newbie, Anne R. Key!" Jesse called over the loudspeaker.

Annie sprinted around the track, bending down low and leaning into the corners as she flew around. A few crossovers later, the pack loomed ahead of her again. *If I can just get by the other blockers once more, I can call off the jam before Mo scores any more points.*

But from where she was, it seemed impossible.

The Derby Dolls were determined not to let Annie pass them again. Lauren was trying hard to create a space for Annie to slip through, but so far she hadn't managed to push any of the Derby Dolls out of bounds.

Two strides before getting to the pack Annie had a brilliant idea. "Lauren," she called. "Leapfrog!"

In a flash, Lauren tucked her head and braced herself in a wide snowplough. Annie picked up some extra speed. In her mind, she was at a gymnastics meet going down the runway and Lauren had turned into a vault. There was no springboard, but no matter. Annie wasn't looking for height and multiple turns in midair. She just needed to clear the vault — something she'd done since she was eight.

Her hands landed square on Lauren's back as she pushed off. Just a basic handspring over the vault. Except as her feet left the ground and she was upside down, Annie remembered this was not gymnastics. The vault was a human, there was no mat beneath her. And she was on skates.

Oh no.

Don't stick the landing, her mind raced. *If I try to stick it, the skates will wipe out from under me and I'll break my bum. Or worse.*

Annie pointed her toes and leaned forward. It was her only hope.

She landed on her toe stops and the momentum dropped her to knees and wrists. Even with the pads that kind of hurt. But not enough to stop a derby girl. She got back on her skates in an instant and glided with her arms in the air, her booty out and back arched.

From the bench, Coach Ritter was frantically flapping her arms at her hips. Annie tapped her hips and called off the jam.

"Dude," Lauren yelled. She wrapped Annie in a tight hug as they both skated off the rink. "That was insane. *You're* insane!"

"I wouldn't have tried it with anyone but you." Annie hugged Lauren back as she glanced around with shocked wide eyes.

The rest of the team hugged them both and Coach Ritter shook her head in disbelief. "Please don't do that again. You almost gave me a heart attack."

"Get used to it." Liz put an arm around Annie when she sat on the bench. "Because this year, the Liberty Belles are going to be full of surprises!"

The crowd, though small, were screaming their

lungs out. Dad was jumping up and down like a five-year-old who'd had too much sugar.

It didn't matter that there were thirty-seven seconds left to the bout. One more jam was played, but no one seemed able to concentrate, let alone score. Not that it mattered. The Liberty Belles were six points ahead when the buzzer sounded to signal the end of the bout.

They did a victory lap around the rink, Liz a bit slower than the rest, and slapped hands with the Derby Dolls and the audience. The Derby Dolls all gave Annie dirty looks as if she had gotten away with something illegal. But she hadn't. She'd read the whole derby rulebook last week and there was nothing that said she couldn't handspring over the pack.

After the Derby Dolls had done their victory lap, Annie skated over to Dad, who was waiting by the side of the rink. Someone, Lexie she guessed, had painted "Anne R. Key" across his forehead like football fans did at home.

Annie's smile spread from ear to ear. One of the best days of her life, for sure.

Dad lifted Annie off her skates in a big hug. "Wow, Beanie. That was amazing. Next time I tell you to be a cheerleader instead, just ignore me. Really. Or tell me to shut up."

Annie buried her head in his shoulder. "I was afraid you weren't going to make it."

"Miss out on something this important to you? Never!" he said before kissing her forehead and putting her down.

"You should be proud." Coach Ritter came up and shook Dad's hand. "I've never seen anything like that before. Or a newbie advance so quickly."

Dad's hand ran through his hair, which made it lie flat for once instead of sticking straight up. He tried to brush off the flour from his shirt but had no luck there. "Annie's always been very determined. When she's good at something, she won't stop until she's risen to the top."

"Does she get that from you?" Coach Ritter asked.

"Good God, no. That's all from her mother. My ex," Dad added quickly as his face turned pink.

Annie cringed a bit at Dad's comment. "Ex" sounded so final. There was still a chance her parents might get back together, right?

She didn't have time to think about that, because Lexie came over and gave her a big hug.

"That was the best thing ever! You couldn't have done that as a cheerleader," Lexie said.

Annie grinned the huge smile she hadn't been able to muster during the cheerleading tryouts.

"This is better than cheerleading," Annie said. She turned toward Jesse, busily putting away the sound system, and added, "For one thing, the music rocks."

"You got that right." He blew the hair out of his gorgeous eyes and flashed her a brilliant smile. Then he said, "You've got to show me how to do the hand-spring thing on wheels. That was sweet!"

"You're on!"

Annie turned back to Lexie, Dad, and Coach Ritter. Dad put his arm around Annie's shoulders, giving them a squeeze.

"If you ever want to become an NSO — non-skating official," Coach Ritter was saying to Dad, "we can always use some extra hands."

Dad nodded, glancing at one of the NSOs in pirate gear, wiping clean the penalty board. "That could be fun," he said. "I can't let Annie have all the glory."

Annie gave her dad a gentle shove. "You just want to wear a funky outfit."

"I get to wear a funky outfit? Dude!" Dad bobbed his head with a cheesy grin. Annie rolled her eyes. Dad was so embarrassing. But she wouldn't trade him for any other.

Lexie, sensing Annie's embarrassment, turned to her. "I'm starving. You guys have any food?"

Dad's head snapped to attention at the sound of his favorite word. "Good thinking. All right, Liberty Belles, back to Rosie Lee's for the after-party."

There was a cheer from the remaining Belles on the rink and they went to tell the girls already getting changed in the locker room. Dad smiled to himself and turned back to Coach Ritter. "Will you come too, Susan?"

Coach Ritter blushed slightly. "Sorry. I have to pick up my kids. From their father's."

"Ah. Well maybe next time." Dad shook the coach's hand.

Did he hold onto it just a smidgen longer than necessary? Nah, Annie was just imagining things. She pushed the thought out of her head as she skated to the locker room.

"Hey, Anne R. Key," a college-aged girl called out. "You were awesome out there. Can't wait to see what else you can do."

"Cheers." Annie waved before going into the locker room. She couldn't wait to see what would happen either.

What a great day. Annie had proven she could be good at something other than gymnastics. She couldn't wait to tell Mum.

Chapter 18

Back at Rosie Lee's, Dad set out a huge plate of the Earl Grey cupcakes Annie and Lexie had invented, along with spiced cookies and chocolate peanut butter brownies. Most of the team had made it, including Lexie, who was definitely an honorary team member. Sadly, Jesse had to work at the rink, so their other honorary member wasn't there.

"I still can't believe you, Annie," Lauren said as she helped herself to another brownie.

"I hope someone caught that on video," Carmen said.

"Where did you learn to do that?" Tashi asked.

Annie didn't know what to say. At that moment it had seemed like the most logical way to get past the pack. Now just the thought that she had done a handspring on skates, over a human, made her wonder if she should get her sanity examined. Still, she couldn't change how amazing it had felt.

"Let's just say I was really, really lucky to pull that off." Annie grinned as she licked the icing off her cupcake. She knew that if she'd touched any other player while her feet were air in the air, the daring move would have got her a major penalty.

"Well, we're really lucky to have all of you on the team," Liz said, determined not to play favorites.

"Watch out, Holly, Annie just might take your place as the team's best jammer," Sharmila said as she hid her face behind a mug of sweet tea.

Holly stuck her tongue out at Sharmila good-naturedly, but Annie had the feeling the comment stung more than she was willing to admit. "Just you wait," Holly retorted. "I'll do a double axel over the pack one of these days. You guys don't need your heads, right?"

The team booed at Holly, who laughed and play-fully threw her napkin at them.

Liz raised her glass of the "champagne" Dad had mixed up: white grape juice and fizzy water. "Here's to the best team the Liberty Belles have ever had. We couldn't have won today without *any* of you."

"Hear, hear!" They all cheered and laughed. Annie couldn't help grinning. It had been a long time since she'd been part of a crowd that really made her feel like she belonged. She doubted the cheerleading squad would have been as welcoming. Not with Kelsey as queen bee.

"Ooh, check it. The whole soccer team is walk-ing by." Sharmila pointed out the window.

Annie jerked around so quickly, she knocked over her glass. Thankfully it was empty and it didn't break. Sure enough, there was Tyler walking by the café with some of his teammates. He looked like he'd just gotten out of the shower, comb marks still visible in his wet hair. Annie wanted nothing more than to mess it up.

Of course. There had been a game tonight. By the cheers the roller girls could hear coming from outside the café, the soccer team must have won. There were some girls laughing and hanging out with them too. Cheerleaders mostly, Annie recognized them. Including Kelsey.

Not that it mattered. Tyler turned at that very moment. His green eyes landed on her brown ones and he burst into a huge smile.

"Yo, Ann-nie!" He held out a hand and waved from the other side of the glass.

Everyone — roller girls, soccer players, and cheerleaders — turned to stare at Annie. Any other time she would have ducked under the table and not come out until she was twenty. But not tonight. Tonight she had vaulted over the pack and helped win the game for her team. Tonight was her night.

She waved back and even though her cheeks were a bit pink, she sent him a smile that matched his.

The cheerleaders gave Annie a dirty look as the soccer team hooted and dragged Tyler away. Before they turned the corner, Tyler looked over his shoulder and waved one last time.

Annie's teammates, who had been watching the exchange in silence, burst into wild giggling. Dad poked his head out of the kitchen with a blob of dough in his hands before rolling his eyes and retreating back to the safety of knives and hot ovens.

"Yo, Ann-nie," Sharmila imitated Tyler's tone exactly. "Will you marry me?"

"Dang, girl. He's only the hottest guy in school," Carmen teased.

A few other girls started making kissing noises.

Annie blushed more now than she had when Tyler had called her name loud enough for the whole street to hear. "Oh, shut it."

"Whatever, you love it." Holly flicked some of her crumbs in Annie's direction.

Annie swatted them away and grinned sheepishly. "Yeah, I kind of do."

"You're so lucky. I'd give anything to go out with him," Cookie sighed.

Annie saw her moment. Even though Cookie seemed to think it was a done deal, Annie had to know for sure. "Isn't he going out with anyone, then?"

"Who would?" Lexie mumbled.

"Not me." Lauren folded her arms over her chest.

Annie narrowed her eyes. Of course Lexie would say that. She hated jocks. But Lauren grew up in a family of jocks. Why would she hate Tyler?

Annie brushed it away. That wasn't important right now. Not when Carmen answered her question.

"Tyler broke up with his girlfriend over the summer." Carmen looked at Annie with a smirk. "Looks like you've got a chance."

The girls cheered and continued to tease Annie. But she didn't care. She had a chance with Tyler. A few weeks ago, she would have never thought it was possible.

I love it here!

Dad put the kettle on when they got home, while Annie rushed to the computer to see if there was any chance Mum might still be awake. The Skype icon said she was, so Annie called her right away.

"Aw, Mum, you should have been there, it was brilliant!" she said. "It was the first time they played me as jammer. There was no way around or through so I had to go over with a handspring. You should have seen the looks on the other team's faces when I flew over them."

Mum pushed up her glasses and frowned as she stared intently at the screen. "What do you mean you did a handspring over some girl's back? Didn't you tell me roller derby is played on skates?"

"Yeah —" Annie started, but she was cut off.

"That sounds very dangerous, sweetheart. You shouldn't take such risks."

Annie sighed. Doing front tucks on the balance beam had been okay but vaulting on skates was dangerous. Whatever.

"It was fine. Really."

Mum shook her head. "I worry about you. If something happened to you being so far away, I . . . Why don't you come back? It would be so nice having you here again. Your room is just how you left it."

Annie looked around Aunt Julie's old room. She had finally started to make it look more like a modern teenager's room with posters of her favorite bands, some artwork by Lexie, and the team photo of the Illinoisies she had printed off the internet. On the bedside table was a picture of Dad, Mum, and herself laughing. The photo was a few years old; Annie must have been around ten.

Realistically, she knew her parents probably wouldn't get back together.

"I've had my ups and downs, I know, but I'm really starting to fit in. Besides, I'm not a quitter, Mum. I got that from you."

Mum smiled, a mixture of pride and sadness. "I guess I did something right, then. Well, I'm off to bed."

"Night, Mum."

Annie moved the mouse to end the call when Mum spoke up again. "Oh, Annie? That room is a mess. Please pick up those clothes I see on the floor."

Annie rolled her eyes and laughed. "Love you, Mum."

"Love you too."

Annie sat by the computer for a couple of seconds, looking around the room some more. She wasn't just saying it. She did like it here. Very much. With a smile, she threw her clothes into a pile in the corner and went to the living room. She found Dad waiting for her with a cup of tea.

"I liked your teammates," he said. "They're a good bunch."

Annie let the steam rise over her face as she breathed deeply. Dad had broken down and bought good quality tea for the house. "I like them too," she said.

Dad's eyes glowed. "And you were so amazing out there. Now I can see why you like roller derby so much. I'm really proud of you."

Annie set down her tea and smiled at him. "I'm proud of you too, Dad. I mean look at Rosie Lee's. It's your dream and it's come true."

"Indeed, indeed." Dad stretched out on the couch and closed his eyes. For a second, Annie thought he'd fallen asleep, until he said, "Yup, I do think this derby thing is not that bad after all."

Annie couldn't resist the opportunity to tease Dad. "Does your change of heart have anything to do with how pretty Coach Ritter is?"

Dad opened his eyes and feigned innocence. "I didn't even notice."

"You were totally checking her out," Annie teased.

Dad sat up, his cheeks a rosy pink. He so rarely got embarrassed that Annie realized she was right. "Listen to you, sounding all American."

Now it was Annie's turn to blush. She hadn't intended to sound American — it just came out that way. Still, she could work with that for now. "Shucks. Sure looks like it, partner. Might jus' have to stick 'round these here parts, keep you in line."

Dad laughed and clinked his mug against hers. "We make a good team, String Bean, don't we?"

"The best!"

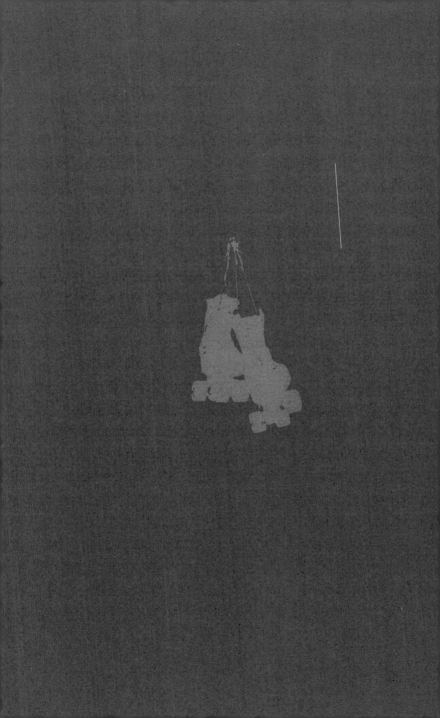